An

Inconvenient

Death

Cyberworld Publishing

www.cyberworldpublishing.com

ISBN 978-1-921879-50-0

Cyberworld Publishing
Jindalee St
Toronto, Australia

Books By Olivia Stowe

Charlotte Diamond Mysteries

By the Howling

Retired With Prejudice

Coast to Coast

An Inconvenient Death

Other books

Fiddler's Rest

Spirit of Christmas

Chatham Square

An

Inconvenient

Death

Olivia Stowe

Chapter One: Hopewell on the Choptank

"Are you upset?"

"No, certainly not," Charlotte said, turning what she hoped was a game face to Brenda Boynton.

"I knew I'd said I was out of the movies, but . . ."

"But Howard Holton sent you a script you couldn't turn down."

Brenda Boynton, Brenda Brandon in films, had retreated—more escaped—to her family home, an eighteenth-century mixed Georgian and federal manse-style house in the small riverside town of Hopewell on Maryland's Choptank River, more than a year ago. There she had found the recently retired senior FBI investigator, Charlotte Diamond, and, eventually had fallen to Charlotte's unusual charms and into her arms.

"Well, yes, but it was more than Howard."

"Your perpetual leading man, David Runion, ganged up with Howard, did he?"

"More like ganged up with Tony Trice," Brenda answered, turning her head away and looking into the sunset across the Choptank. They were sitting, bundled up in the chill of the late October evening next to a chimenea, with smoldering fire, by the dock at the back of Brenda's house—now Charlotte's too—drinking wine and reviewing the events of their day. Rocket, their boxer, lay, contentedly panting, by Brenda's chair just as Sam, their Siberian husky, took up the position next to Charlotte's chair. The women had been gone most of the day, and the dogs had stuck closely to their sides ever since they'd come back from Washington, D.C.

"Ah, when a son calls, a mother will answer," Charlotte said softly, looking out beyond the pier to give Brenda her privacy. Brenda and David Runion had been a screen couple for couples—and were perhaps the leading couple in the movie houses in their generation. Brenda waited, without success, most of that time for Runion to look her way. But, Tinseltown rumors aside, when Brenda had recently acknowledged to a few that the heartthrob actor of their ensemble, Tony Trice, was her son, she also had to included the declaration that he wasn't Runion's son. Everyone seemed to assume that Brenda and David were a couple off screen as well as on. For years Brenda had kept the existence of her out-of-wedlock son, born before she went to Hollywood and became a star, secret. But she had kept tabs on him as he grew up, and when she saw that he had a talent for acting, she's arranged for him to come to Los Angeles and to become part of the Runion-Brandon film dynasty.

Brenda and Tony had only acknowledged that they knew they were mother and son during the recent film shoot in Hollywood where

Charlotte had been instrumental in clearing Brenda of the murder of her former lover. Since that time, Brenda hadn't felt she was able to do enough for her son.

"I wouldn't have to say yes, of course," Brenda continued. "It's a rather interesting film. Aaron Woolridge—he's producing again, naturally—uncovered an unsolved mystery of a murder and disappearances during the filming of a war propaganda film in central Florida during the early seventies—during the Vietnam War. The movie companies almost all had film studios there then, did you know? And, actually, Charlotte, although they do want me to do a minor part in the movie, what Aaron really wants is for you to look at the mystery and to help in the writing of the script."

"Me?" Charlotte said, surprised. She sat up in the Adirondack chair, or, more precisely, perhaps, shifted her bulk toward the front of the chair, nearly knocking over the wine bottle that had been resting by the chair leg and causing Sam to woof and move a few inches away from her—probably in fear of being crushed if she couldn't keep her balance.

"Yes, he was very impressed with how you helped handle Helga's murder case—and with exposing John Lu. Of course, he laughed about that and said you owed him a scriptwriter since you took John away from him. He'd like you to come down to Florida too and help them put together a scenario for the original crime—one that they can build a movie script on. But, I know, I'd said I'd had my fill of films."

"It's not the film, Brenda. Honestly, it's not. In March when you say they wanted you down there, I'll be winter crazy here, I know, and ready for some warmer weather. Yes, you must do it, and I'll latch onto any excuse to going down there with you. And I'll think about consulting on the scripting if Aaron genuinely needs the help and you aren't just trying to find a way to make me fit in down there. There's nothing wrong. I'm just tired from the weekend in D.C."

"You don't see your brother all that much. But you seemed to have gotten along with him well today at lunch at Guapo's. And I found his wife, Marilyn quite vivacious. I would never have guessed she was a minister."

"Few do guess that," Charlotte answered, with a laugh. "You should see that woman shop." But then it seemed like Charlotte's voice had caught on that last statement, and she turned her head so that Brenda couldn't see her frown.

"Perhaps I shouldn't have suggested we meet for lunch while we were both in Washington this weekend—it just seemed so fortuitous, your brother and his wife attending that convocation at the American University seminary and you going to that award ceremony at FBI Headquarters Saturday night."

"No, no, that was fine. As you say, I don't see Chance often. He's busy with his medical practice down in Williamsburg. We've both been living on the East Coast most of our lives, but until I retired from the FBI, I was as busy with my job as he was with his. We have rarely had the opportunity to get together. That was nice, a nice lunch. I wished you could have gone with me to the award ceremony and dinner afterward, though."

"You know how it is, Charlotte. It's nothing I ask for, but I can't seem to go anywhere without becoming the center of attention—

and the award ceremony was for you and the others. The distraction would have unfair to you. And I always have old friends and colleagues to catch up with in Washington—and members of Congress to give a piece of my mind to."

"Yes, but I would have liked to have you by my side. I don't want to shy away from people seeing the two of us together. There's no shame in having found each other. Especially at our ages—well, mine, if not yours."

Brenda laughed. "You are too sensitive about the age difference, Charlotte. It's only a couple of years. And, as you say, at our age . . ."

"You'll always look glamorous and luminous, Brenda. And I'll always look like a laundry bag the day before washing day."

"Not so," Brenda remonstrated. "More wine?" She was holding up the wine bottle.

"I guess we'd better finish it up, yes, and get inside. It's getting dark and the fire's almost out—and it looks like a storm might be brewing up the river from the Chesapeake."

Brenda made to rise from her chair, but when she looked over and saw that Charlotte hadn't tossed off the wine Brenda had poured into her glass but was still pensively staring out over the river, she settled again. Rocket raised on his haunches and put his head in her lap and she started petting him.

Although it wasn't what was primarily bothering her at the moment, Charlotte was quite serious about regretting that Brenda hadn't been beside her at the awards ceremony and dinner the previous evening. She was serious about wanting to declare to the world that she and Brenda were a couple. And more than to the world, she wanted to make that quite clear to Evan Worthington, an old flame and the new chief of the Annapolis FBI office, who had arrived there after Charlotte had retired but who subsequently told her he had taken the post to be near her. He had been at her side at the awards ceremony the previous evening—and then, again, was nearly plastered to her side at dinner.

"Come back to work, Charlotte. We need you in Annapolis," he had said.

And when she had laughed and demurred and said that he had an excellent crew in Annapolis—that she'd trained many of them herself, he'd put his hand on her arm and said, "Well come back to me in Annapolis, please. I can't get along without you."

"I'm about to leave on a long vacation floating down the Rhine for Christmas, Evan. You will have found someone else twice as worthy as me before I get back."

"Never," he had whispered.

"And I'm with Brenda Boynton now, Evan. I've made no secret of that. I've made a completely new life for myself."

"Yes, you certainly seem to have," he'd said with a laugh. "But I can always hope."

"Something you'll have to do on your own time and with your own energy, I'm afraid," Charlotte had said. But saying it was a whole lot easier than actually believing it. Evan had been her first fall-over-your-heels love. She had lost him to another woman and then moved on to an unsatisfactory marriage that she had tried to make work for decades. But when Evan's wife had died, he had come back looking for Charlotte. And she couldn't say totally that she was over him yet. She had assumed she was—but that was when she thought he was safely removed from her, married and on another continent. She couldn't tell Brenda that there were residual feelings for a man, of course. Brenda was the best thing that had ever happened to Charlotte. She still couldn't fully believe that the gorgeous movie star—both in mind and body—had been attracted to her.

The reappearance of Evan was enough to knock Charlotte off her pins—and this was the biggest reason she'd agreed to taking the two-week trip with Brenda at Christmas to cruise down the Rhine—but this wasn't the main reason she was reticent this evening.

"I still don't know what's causing you to run so silent, Charlotte. Is it because I told Chance and Marilyn that they should come with us on the Rhine trip? I did notice that you gave a little start at that."

"Bingo," Charlotte thought. But what she said was. "No, of course not. That's fine. I think Chance and Marilyn are better in small doses, yes, but the four of us seemed to get along just fine at dinner. I haven't traveled with Chance for years, though. The Rhine might not be the best place . . ."

Charlotte couldn't finish the sentence.

"I'm sorry. I didn't realize that there was any strain between you and Chance," Brenda said. "I certainly want this vacation to be a real vacation for you—relaxing. Remember, we were considering the most out-of-character vacations when we came up with this. To escape from everything for a week or two."

"Yes, I remember, and I'm afraid that's rather the point. It isn't that there's any strain between Chance and me. We've always gotten along perfectly well."

"Well, what is it, then—If it's something you can verbalize and feel comfortable telling me?"

"I feel comfortable telling you anything," Charlotte said, with a smile—a smile that turned slightly into a grimace and another glance away as she remembered that she certainly didn't want to discuss Evan Worthington with Brenda. But she looked right back at Brenda, determined to tell her what was on her mind.

"It's not anything between Chance and me. And it's not Marilyn, either, if that's what you're thinking. I find her funny and refreshing, and if she's a bit zany—and very hard to imagine as a minister—it's just a bit more added to her charm. It's going on a vacation with Chance."

"Going on a vacation? I don't understand."

"Chance is a doctor."

"Yes, and?"

"And every time I'm with him for more than a week at a time, someone dies—not often someone we know, thank goodness—although, lord knows, that's happened too. But someone drops dead and Chance winds up stuck with playing doctor and filling out forms and such. And if Marilyn is there, her time and effort is taken up with ministering to the bereaved. All sense of a vacation goes flying out of the window."

"Oh, I'm sure it doesn't always happen. But I can see why that would give you pause. It's not much of a vacation for you if people are dying around you, I guess."

"An eleven-day cruise. Three bodies. I can almost guarantee it."

"Oh, go on with you," Brenda said, with a laugh. "Now you're just having me on. I don't see Chance Diamond as the grim reaper. And, I'm sure it doesn't matter anyway. The cruise is only seven weeks away. If he's as busy as you say with his practice, I'm sure there isn't time for him to get away—and the cruise is probably booked up anyway."

"Ah, but you didn't see the expression on Marilyn's face when you suggested it. That's what made me look apprehensive at lunch."

"Marilyn's face?"

"You mentioned the trip in the same sentence with Christmas markets along the Rhine. Marilyn is a champion shopper. They *will* be going on that cruise with us. That's another guarantee I can make."

"Well, Miss Gloom and Doom. It's dark now and that wine bottle is empty and I will be going into the house now. And it's straight to bed for me. As you've already noted, it's been an exhausting weekend. Are you coming or staying out here wrapped up in your cocoon and watching Sam's and Rocket's breath crystallize in the air?"

"Going inside and straight to bed? Of course I'm coming in with you." And Charlotte gave Brenda "that" look, which caused Brenda to give the throaty laugh and twinkling eye effect that had moved theatergoers to warm thoughts for decades. As the last vestiges of the reddish-orange sun sank below the tree line on west bank of the

Choptank, the two women, flanked by two happily panting pooches, marched off comfortably, arm in arm, to their bed.

Chapter Two: Day One: München to Nürnberg

"How very extraordinarily amusing," Brenda said as she and Charlotte walked out of the airport terminal at München's Franz Josef Strauss International Airport behind Dietrich Hahn, who had been introduced to them in the baggage claim area as their tour guide for the next eleven days. Ahead of them, causing them to shuffle along slowly, huffed a young man struggling with a baggage cart piled high with their luggage. Hahn had introduced the man, calling him "our crewman from Spain," merely as Rico. Behind them strolled the Melards, Doris and Malcolm, who had been on the same plane with them from Philadelphia but who only now were identified as being on the same tour they were on. Doris seemed to prefer the slow pace that Charlotte and Brenda were finding too ponderous and was leaning heavily on her husband's arm.

"Extraordinary, yes, that Chance and Marilyn managed to get here at the same place but ahead of us despite leaving from Dulles later than we did and on a later-scheduled flight. But hardly amusing."

Charlotte wasn't amused by anything concerning air travel. They'd taken business class, but she didn't have even a business-class superstructure. She vaguely wondered whether first class even would be comfortable for her. It wasn't just her girth; Charlotte was a tall, big-boned woman by anyone's standards.

"When I said 'extraordinary,' I didn't mean your brother and Marilyn, Charlotte. Look at that tableau at the bus stop under that awning over there where Chance is standing."

Charlotte looked and then she did have to chuckle. There was a small bench under the awning, and sitting primly on the seat were a Japanese couple, looking to be in their late thirties, he on one end, and she on the other—and between them, taking up most of the space and with an arm each of the couple protectively encircling it, was a large, garishly dressed Cabbage Patch doll. This brand of doll was of a large, floppy variety, the early ones, like this, having a vinyl head and cloth body, that had been the rage decades earlier. The gimmick of the doll was that each came out of the factory with its own name and a birth certificate—the combination of which jacked the price of the doll up a good fifty dollars.

The image of a rag doll being treated almost like someone's child was amusing enough, but overlaying this were the two elderly ladies—certainly more in need of the bench than either the younger Japanese couple or their rag doll—who were standing facing the bench. The two women reminded Charlotte instantly of the nursery rhyme about Jack Sprat and his wife because of the differences in their stature—which proved to be quite prophetic, as Chance subsequently gave them those nicknames as well. One of the habits that Chance unabashedly irritated his younger sister with was assigning nicknames to the people he met. Charlotte, almost ashamedly, realized when she heard him call them the same thing that she had picked up his habit. Chance already was referring to Brenda as the Goddess. And Charlotte seethed at Chance's insistence since childhood to call his younger sister Droopydrawers, for no reason Charlotte could think of other than it often got a rise from her and a lifting of the eyebrows from those around them who heard him use the term.

It wasn't just the physical size of the two women that made Charlotte think of them as cartoonish opposites—one woman was tall and thin as a rail, whereas the other was short and fat—it was their demeanor as well. The taller woman was leaning down toward the Cabbage Patch doll and smiling. cooing at it, and chucking it under the chin as if it really were a baby, while the shorter, fat, woman, who was leaning on a cane, was standing at judgmental attention and giving the Japanese couple a hard, disapproving stare.

Both Charlotte and Brenda were still chuckling when they came up beside Chance and Marilyn.

"Enjoying our little tableau of the Couple Sprat in the Orient?" Chance asked in the way of a greeting of his sister and friend, who he had last seen seven weeks earlier on the East Coast of the United States.

Charlotte gave him a hard look, surprised, of course, that he had nailed the two elderly women with exactly the image she had formed, but also because the Jack Sprat comparison was one that was a sore point with her already where it concerned Chance Diamond. The sister and brother couldn't have been more different than if they'd

19

sprung from different sides of the earth. Whereas Charlotte was tall and statuesque—in the words of those who wanted to be as polite as possible to her—and felt each crumb she ate gravitating immediately to her hips, Chance, although certainly tall, wasn't as tall as Charlotte, looked like the distinguished professional that he was, and could eat a deep-fried elephant without gaining an ounce of fat where it would show on his frame. And, Charlotte was painfully aware, Chance had come blessed with more grace and beauty than she ever could dream of having. Her older brother was gregarious and made friends easily; Charlotte was reticent and people were scared of her. Of course, since most of the people she had spent a lot of time with in her life were hardened criminals she was tracking down and putting behind bars, the fear came naturally to many of her relationships. The only attribute in which they could claim any form of common ground and equality was that each was smart as a whip and highly respected professionals.

Apparently Chance and Marilyn had been standing beside the bus that was to take them from München to Nürnberg, where they all would embark on their ship for the cruise from the Main River to the Rhine and then on to Amsterdam. They were still standing on the pavement, because the bus had been locked while their tour guide, Dietrich Hahn, and his helper, Rico—who was soon revealed as the bus driver—met their flight.

Charlotte would have liked to have gotten on the bus immediately upon Rico having unlocked the door before starting to manhandle the luggage into the compartment at the bottom of the bus, but Chance was too busy introducing himself to the couple that had flown in with Charlotte and Brenda and in insisting that his sister

20

meet them as well. "Also," he said, "I like to watch until I'm absolutely sure my luggage is going with me."

Charlotte was hopping from one foot to the other, trying to stay warm and muttering under her breath to Brenda how wintry cold it was and asking why they had chosen to go to the frozen tundra on their vacation.

"Germany's hardly the frozen tundra, darling," Brenda responded, flashing that sparkly smile of hers. "If that temperature sign over there is to be believed, it's two degrees warmer here now than it was when we left Hopewell—and, remember, we wanted a vacation that contrasted with anything else we would have done this time of year. Christmas in Germany is going to be divine."

"Christmas in the village markets along the river is going to be divine," Marilyn chirped in.

"My goodness, you couldn't be Brenda Brandon, the movie star?" interjected Doris Melard, suddenly very animated and very much alive.

When Charlotte had seen the woman in passing by her in the airplane on one of the walks Charlotte had taken to try to get the circulation going in her legs again, she had wondered if the woman was well. Her aspect was ashen and she seemed to be palsied. She was trembling and slack-jawed, and her eyes looked like they were in pain. But now she looked dazzled to be in the presence of just-discovered movie royalty.

"Guilty as charged, I'm afraid," Brenda answered. "But on this trip I'm merely Brenda Boynton, ready to stand in awe of quaint, snow-covered German villages and majestic castles along the Rhine with everyone else. But, surely, I do believe, I've met you before. But Melard, you say? That name doesn't seem to ring a bell."

"Perhaps you knew me as Pease or Hendricks. I recently was married to Peter Hendricks, the manufacturer of—"

"No, Pease it is, I think. The mustard people. I attended a premier of one of my movies in Philadelphia, and you were there. Your father is—was, I guess—the condiment manufacturer and philanthropist, Jonathan Pease, if I remember rightly."

"Well, yes, he was," Mrs. Melard said, a blush having come to her cheeks, the first sign of health Charlotte had seen in her. As it was, she was still leaning heavily on her husband's arm. And her husband wasn't looking at Brenda—his eyes were boring into Charlotte—and it was Charlotte he addressed.

"But you aren't in the movies too, are you, Miss . . . ?"

"No, no, I'm just a retired policewoman. And you've met my brother, Chance, and his wife, I think, already. Chance is a physician in Williamsburg, Virginia, and Marilyn is a—"

"I think you must be far too modest," the man interrupted her. "I thought I recognized you in the baggage claim area, but now that your brother has been introduced under the name Diamond, I'm sure. You're the famous FBI investigator, Charlotte Diamond, aren't you?"

"Hardly famous."

"Well, to me you are. I'm Malcolm Melard. I teach at the Wharton School in Philadelphia. Economics, but my specialty is international financial crime. You're rather a legend on the East Coast, you know. You come up in several of the cases I teach in my courses."

"Ones where the good guys won, I hope," Charlotte said, with a shy little smile. She wasn't used to being singled out like this—especially when Brenda was nearby.

"But of course. You won every one of the cases I use in my classes," Professor Melard said, with admiration. And as he said that, the Japanese couple brushed by the group of six and the Japanese man looked up, startled, at Professor Melard. Charlotte noted this, as it seemed a strange reaction. Melard hadn't stood in the couple's way or anything.

Charlotte looked over to the bench, where she was pleased to see that the two elderly ladies now had been able to sit. The tall, thin one had a handkerchief laid over her lap and some sort of brocade jewelry case sitting on the bench beside her and was showing several pieces of antique jewelry to the short, stout woman with the cane, who was still wearing her scowl even though the Japanese couple had finally relinquished the bench to her.

The Japanese man came down from the bus and, making a wide swath around the discussion group Charlotte was in, started yammering at Rico and pulling suitcases back from underneath the bus as fast as Rico was stowing them in. Rico was trying to find out what the Japanese man wanted, but he just kept digging until the suitcases once more were strewn across the sidewalk and up against the bench, jostling the elderly women and making them scoot to one side. At last the Japanese man seemed to have found what he wanted, though, and turning first to Rico, who was squashed up against the tall, thin lady, and giving him deep-waisted bow and then, making another one, to the elderly ladies, nearly toppling them back off the bench, he turned and scurried back onto the bus. He now was clutching a sweater he had pulled out of a suitcase to his chest. Giving a slight "the things we do for the tourists" shrug of his shoulders and a shy smile to the elderly women, Rico returned to doing what he'd already done—packing in a mountain of luggage in the bus's baggage compartment.

But now at last, Dietrich Hahn was back from the terminal with the last couple he needed to collect for the bus ride to the river boat in Nürnberg, Rico was stashing the last bit of luggage in the vehicle's compartments, and Hahn was good-naturedly trying to shepherd those standing outside the bus to get on. Charlotte needed no convincing. She felt like an icicle, and, although she, like the others were politely standing aside to let the two elderly ladies get on the bus first, she didn't wait on ceremony to be right behind them.

The Japanese couple had taken up the front seats on both side of the aisle, the woman to the left, behind the driver, in one seat, with her carryon bags and those of her husband in the seat next to her, even though Dietrich had clearly told everyone to put their carryons in the overhead bins. Her husband sat at the window on the other side, and next to him, in the only seat on the bus with room for someone to stretch their legs, sat the Cabbage Patch doll.

Charlotte was held up on the steps up into the bus by what seemed to be a small set-to involving the elderly ladies—or, the short, stout one, to be precise—and the couple taking up the four front seats.

"But I need room to stretch my leg out straight," the short, stout elderly lady was whining, as she stood over the Cabbage Patch doll and looked almost ready to hit a home run with it's head with her cane.

24

"Yoo hoo, back here, Hattie," the tall, thin elderly lady was calling from half way back in the bus. "I'm sure you will have enough leg room here."

The belligerent Hattie person was ignoring the summery-tempered other elderly woman, though, and was trying to stare down the Cabbage Patch doll. The doll wasn't showing any interest or remorse, nor did either of the Japanese when Hattie turned her ire on them. They just sat there and smiled and shrugged a "no speaka dee English" universal response.

There was quite a backup behind Charlotte, and those who had no idea what the holdup was were leaning forward and pressing against Charlotte to the point that she almost toppled into Hattie.

Finally seeing that her remonstrations were going to do no good, the short, stout elderly lady finally gave up and, after muttering something under her breath that Charlotte very much thought a lady of that age shouldn't even know the meaning of, she humphed back to the seat that the other woman was trying to, at least visually, make as comfy as possible.

On the nearly two-hour bus ride from Münich to the pier at Nürnberg, the group of six—Charlotte and her three companions and the Melards—having found seats within a distance where raised voices would reach over the road noise, Brenda, Marilyn, and Doris Melard carried on one conversation about what there was to buy and see—mainly buy—in Germany at Christmastime—reduced eventually to mostly Brenda and Marilyn as Doris visibly faded from the exertion. Simultaneously, Charlotte, Chance, and Professor Melard spoke of medical crimes, concentrating on deaths by natural causes that weren't so natural. Melard had latched onto Chance's medical background and brought that into the discussion by way of a case of Charlotte's he used in his class where a Ponzi scheme shyster had been found dead in his minimum security cell just a few weeks previously. Many failed investors had called for his execution, they'd been so worked up by his schemes at the time, and Melard wanted to know from Chance how easy it would have been for one of those investors to reach out to harm the shyster and from Charlotte whether she thought that might be the case.

Charlotte didn't think there was a connection between his death and the calls for his death by bilked investors, but she was trapped in a bus, the countryside was dreary this time of year—the sky was a gloomy gray and it had started to rain—and she didn't mind reminiscing about one of her own cases. She would have gladly rung the arrogant and grasping Ponzi schemer's neck herself at the time of the investigation and trial, given half a chance. She didn't feel much sympathy for most of the people he'd bilked, though. They were all trying to get rich fast on a scheme that they should have known was too good to be true.

Near the end of the bus ride, Charlotte noticed out of the corner of her eye that the sunny version of the two elderly ladies was now a bit agitated. She was up out of her seat and fiddling around in the overhead bin and then in the corners of her vacated seat.

"I'm sure you put it in your luggage before that Spaniard loaded up the baggage compartment on the bus, Irene," Charlotte overheard the short, stout one saying. "Check when we get to the boat. You'll find it there. I swear you'd forget your nose if it wasn't sown on your face. And stop this fidgeting; it isn't here."

But just then Professor Melard was pointing out that they could see the river boats—three of them, long and sleek—through the raindrops, and Charlotte, like everyone else, was turning her attention to what would be their floating home for the next week and a half. At the request of several, Dietrich Hahn pointed out the boat that was theirs. Her name was the *Rhine Maiden*, and she'd been commissioned less than a year before. She wasn't the longest boat at the dock, but she was beautiful, long, and gleaming white. It was hard for Charlotte and the others to believe that there were three decks in the interior and that the 280-foot, narrow beam craft was capable of carrying and serving 100 passengers plus crew in luxury.

That's also the moment that Charlotte remembered that she'd always hated ships and being out on the ocean as opposed to on the river in her one-person Penguin—despite Brenda's many remonstrations that a river was a river and not the ocean—and began to feel nauseous, seasickness already setting in when the river was hardly in view yet. Why, she thought for the umpteenth time, had she capitulated this easily on taking this winter river cruise vacation? Oh, yeah, she then remembered. Something about getting beyond the attraction and seduction of Evan Worthington.

* * * *

There were only six suites on the *Rhine Maiden*, although, when booking, Charlotte and Brenda had been told that all of the cabins were oversized for a boat of this nature, whose dimensions were set by the size of the many locks they would have to go through on the Main and upper Rhine. There were a good many cruise ships on the rivers longer than the *Rhine Maiden*, but she was as wide as any of the others. The ship had fifty passenger cabins in all, going down the three interior decks in price and size. That there were only six suites, all on the upper level, was because the restaurant, the Lorelei, aft of the first-class suites, and the reception desk foyer and the bar cum lounge, Neptune's, forward of the suites, were all on the same level. And the restaurant and lounge were large enough to serve the entire ship.

Once there, Charlotte thought this was a rather bad arrangement, as it meant that people would be traipsing back and forth on the corridor the suites were on when going from restaurant to lounge, but Brenda had insisted on splurging, and she said that surely the soundproofing would be good in the corridor walls. In this, she was proven correct, although both she and Charlotte came to wish that the same soundproofing had gone into the walls between the cabins.

The suites took up the space of two of the next-lower-class cabins on the deck below them—and room was tight enough even in the suites that Charlotte didn't even want to contemplate the size of the cabins on the lowest deck. She couldn't complain about how the space was being used efficiently, however, and she would have enjoyed the major feature of the suite—that it had a French balcony—if only it wasn't the dead of winter and she could stand there and count the icicles dripping from the top of the sliding-glass-door frame.

The suites were in two sets of three, positioned across from each other. Charlotte and Brenda had the suite nearest the restaurant on the port side, with Chance and Marilyn Diamond in the suite nearest the reception area and the lounge on the same side, Chance having booked too late to get a cheaper cabin. It was a mystery until sometime after they sailed who had the cabin between them.

The Melards were in the suite across the corridor from Chance and Marilyn, and, much to Charlotte's chagrin and Brenda's amusement, the Japanese couple with the Cabbage Patch doll had the cabin across from them. It was late in the afternoon, near sundown, when Charlotte found out who the middle cabin on the other side was assigned to—and then only because she was standing at the sliding glass doors and counting the icicles when a black Mercedes limousine pulled up very close to the gangplank and two uniformed chauffeurs jumped out of the front and one held a backseat passenger door open and the other scurried around to the trunk and began unloading a mountain of luggage.

"Ah, this should be real fun," Charlotte said with a little laugh as she saw who stepped out of the limousine first. The Swiss banker Hans Eberhardt's photograph had been tacked to one of the bulletin boards in the investigations room at the Annapolis FBI office for several years while Charlotte had been working there. There was no special reason it was in that particular office; it probably was on a cork board somewhere in every investigations room in every FBI office in the world. They'd been after this one for years because of his money-laundering activities for known terrorists, tinhorn dictators of third world countries, and other assorted thieves. "Malcolm Melard will salivate over this one."

"What do you see?" Brenda asked, drawn from where she had been reclining on the bed and reading a novel, to the window, where Charlotte had the draperies pulled aside. "Oh, who is that with Sophia Fazy?"

"Sophia who?" Charlotte had been concentrating on Eberhardt, but now she saw that a woman, a couple of decades younger than Eberhardt and three times as pretty, had climbed out of the back of the limousine.

"Sophia Fazy. She's an Italian television actress—known more for her superstructure than her talent, I might add, if you won't tell anyone before I can retract my claws. I'd heard she'd married some rich old banker."

"That would probably be the man on the gangplank ahead of her," Charlotte said. "That's Hans Eberhardt, a Swiss banker. And if you run into him this week on the ship, I strongly suggest you hold on tight to your purse."

A commotion in the hall—loud enough to defeat the insulation—and the sound of luggage bumping against walls confirmed to Charlotte that she now knew who was booked into the middle suite across the corridor.

Several minutes after the noise had abated, Charlotte walked over to the bed Brenda had returned to and leaned down and gave her a sweet kiss on the lips. "Harvey Wallbanger time for me. Would you like to accompany me to see what King Neptune has to offer before dinner?"

"I'll bet you don't even know what's in a Harvey Wallbanger."

"Don't care. It's the daily special, and I'm going to try a daily special each day of this cruise. And I don't care what's in them. You've told me we're flinging it all away, letting it all hang out, or whatever, on this vacation. And I feel like living dangerously."

"Well, I do know what's in a Harvey Wallbanger," Brenda said, with a laugh, "and I'll not be having one of those."

"You can live less dangerously but more expensively then. I know you like Daiquiris, and those can be had for just thirty-five cents more."

It turned out that Charlotte liked Harvey Wallbangers just fine—twice—and that she wasn't walking too steady when, after having met up with Chance and Marilyn in the lounge, they were moving toward the dining room for their first aboard-ship dinner.

"Whoa, a little squally on this cruise already," Charlotte complained.

"We're not even getting underway until tomorrow night, Charlotte. The ship's steady as a rock. I can't quite say the same thing for you." And then, as they approached the dining room. "What ho this? Is that Laurel hovering into sight? Is this the only restaurant on this tub?"

As he was finishing, the maitre d', obviously having been well-versed in who the first-class passengers were, was descending down the corridor upon them, all tuxedo-clad stick figure smiles and genuflections. Although Charlotte didn't belie Chance's Laurel nickname—especially after the morose, obese head chef put in an appearance later and promptly earned the name Hardy, thus

31

completing the comedy team of Laurel and Hardy—her first impression of the fawning French-chattering Pierre Pelletier, who she later was to discover had been simply Peter Skinner from the Bronx, was a more horrifying image of the emcee in *Cabaret*.

Making a quick pact, Charlotte, Chance, and Brenda left Marilyn in the grip of Pierre and forged their way across the dining room to a free four-chair table.

"She has several parishioners just like him," Chance murmured as they sidestepped him and left Marilyn to his mercy. "She'll know what to do."

She managed, of course, as any well-trained minister of God would, but she had a few ungodly words to share with Chance for abandoning her when she finally managed her escape and met them at the table. She hadn't been far behind them, as the other three had stopped briefly to gawk at the table set for six where the Japanese couple had taken up residence and were in the process, each with a spoon, of feeding French onion soup to their Cabbage Patch doll. No one else would, of course, be asking permission to occupy any of the three empty chairs at that table.

"Pathetic," Charlotte muttered, as she sat in her chair and reached for the wine list.

"Probably more tragic," Marilyn said, having leveled her husband in three sharp strokes of her tongue and settled in her chair.

"How so?" Charlotte asked, knowing that they both were referencing the behavior of the Japanese couple, which considerably more bizarre than the behavior of Pierre the maitre d', as hard as that was to fathom.

"Unfortunately, I've seen that before. Maybe not that pronounced. They probably both have wanted children for years and for some reason—his impotency or her barrenness—they've recently discovered that isn't going to happen. They likely believe they are past the age to adopt. It's overcompensation. It probably won't last long. They'll either divorce, each blaming the other one, or they will bite the bullet and adopt regardless of their ages."

"Sounds far-fetched," Charlotte said, but then she looked past the warning glance from Brenda, telling her not to be starting family issues this early in the cruise, to Chance, who was nodding his head. "Afraid she's right, Droopydrawers. By the end of the cruise they'll probably realize how silly this is. Until they do, I imagine we'll all suffer in some way."

After giving Chance a light, sisterly jab on the arm, Charlotte looked around the room. Her eyes spotted the two elderly ladies, who still seemed to be discussing something that had gone wrong earlier this afternoon—Charlotte couldn't quite remember what it might have been. In any event, the woman who had been so rosy of demeanor earlier looked a little crestfallen, while the short, stout woman was being fussy with the waiter—who was revealed to be the Rico of the bus ride—and was obviously being highly critical of the food or service, or both. Whatever her problem, she was making rather loud and gruff demands. Rico was beside himself trying to please her. There didn't seem to be any pleasing of her to be had, though.

Both the elderly ladies and the Japanese couple had gone to dinner early—the first-class passengers having no restrictions on when they used the dining room—and Charlotte stopped looking around at the other diners when Hans and Sophia Eberhardt put in an appearance at the restaurant's door, making an entrance that was highlighted by yet more fawning and genuflecting by Pierre. She didn't know if Eberhardt would recognize her, but she didn't want to spend the entire cruise with him believing she was there to stalk him.

"Who's for bridge?" Marilyn asked brightly as they were finishing their deserts and their coffee.

No one responded until Chance finally said, "With you, dear, bridge is a contact sport. We've all flown across the pond today. Maybe something less invigorating."

"Well, we could all gather in our cabin and watch the movie they're showing tonight."

"What are they showing?" Charlotte asked.

"*Judgment at Nürnberg*," Brenda answered, almost unable to stifle a giggle.

"Oh god, no," Chance and Charlotte growled together.

"Me, I'm for bed to sleep the sleep of the dead," Charlotte said, as she started shifting her body in the chair in the first stage of a failed attempt to gracefully escape its clutching confines.

"Me too," Chance tossed back at her.

"And me three," Brenda added to the pile.

In the event, none of them were right about getting a good night's sleep.

Chapter Three: Day Two: Nürnberg

The Diamond foursome were a tad touchy and grumpy early the next morning at breakfast in the Lorelei, as were, Charlotte noted, a few of the other cruisers around them who she recognized. The Japanese couple and their "child" seemed chipper enough, although the Cabbage Patch doll seemed to be fussy and resisting her food this morning. But the elderly ladies seemed a little on edge, as did Doris Melard. Charlotte wondered if anyone's spirits would be lifted if Pierre had been there to salivate over them at the restaurant's entrance. Perhaps, she thought, he was only on the entertainment schedule in the evening. She couldn't check on his lunch schedule, as lunch was to be on their own in downtown Nürnberg during a morning and early afternoon in the environs of the Augustinerstrasse Christmas market. This would be one of the largest markets they would be able to visit, because Christmas was only days away and the famous German street markets were beginning to close down. Both Marilyn and Brenda were chomping at the bit to get out onto the shopping streets.

Rico, the young Spaniard with dark-eyed and olive-complexioned matinee idol looks, and a cute young Danish waitress,

Gretchen, who had served Charlotte's table for dinner, were busy hustling around, doing what they could to keep up with the breakfast crowd that would soon need to be on buses to be taken down into the center of the city. Charlotte reached for her coffee cup to see that it hadn't been filled yet. When she turned to see where the wait staff were, she saw that Gretchen was busy commiserating with Doris Melard—who looked quite pale and wan this morning—over something and Rico was being dressed down over a water-stained crystal glass by the short and stout elderly lady. The other woman, so sunny the first time they had seen her, was looking on with a rather listless look on her face.

Thinking that Gretchen might be the first purveyor of coffee to break free, Charlotte tuned her ear in to her conversation with Doris Melard.

"I'm sorry to hear that, Mrs. Melard. You say it went missing in the lounge last night. Your mother's, you say. Emeralds? Oh, my. I trust you reported it to Chris, who was tending bar last night. I'd be happy to ask him about it again after the breakfast service is over."

Misplaced jewelry? Charlotte mused. Who would bring emeralds on a cruise in a foreign country anyway, she wondered. Of course who can safely take any jewelry of value anywhere these days? More of a nuisance than it was worth. She herself had never been a collector of expensive baubles. While thinking on this, she was reminded of the antique jewelry she'd seen one of the elderly ladies showing to the other on the bench at the bus at the München airport the previous day. She wondered if the glum appearance of that previously happy-aspect woman was related to having lost some of that jewelry. The investigator instinct in Charlotte was beginning to rev up.

"How about you, Charlotte?"

"How about me what? Could you repeat that, Marilyn? I'm afraid my mind was elsewhere."

"Chance was just telling Brenda that we got hardly two contiguous hours of sleep last night because we periodically were hearing a bumping noise. I hope it isn't something down in the engine room that we'll have to live with the entire cruise. And Brenda said you were kept awake by such a noise too. We'd go for about an hour of silence and almost get back into a deep sleep, when the bumping noise would start up again and go for about twenty minutes."

"Yes, yes, we were kept awake by that too," Charlotte answered, "and if I don't get some coffee pretty soon, I think I'm going to go on a rampage. You'll all have to stand back as I chew on the table cloth—or I might go for that rhinestone Christmas tree brooch you're wearing."

"They aren't rhinestones, dear. And you'll swallow this over my dead body. Chance gave me this last Christmas when we were touring India."

"I meant to ask you whether traveling in India at Christmas time was a bit strange—especially for a minister," Charlotte answered, as, thankfully, Rico had heard her plea and was doing a tango with the departing Japanese man beside Marilyn's chair as he was trying to get to Charlotte with a pot of coffee. "In fact, you seem to be traveling at Christmas a lot."

"Sermons aren't my thing," Marilyn said. "I'm more the visitation and comforting type. And I found that someone always wanted me to fill in in their pulpit around Christmas time—so Chance and I years ago devised a plan to have me out of circulation then. But funny that you mentioned the India trip last year. We never looked for it, but everywhere we turned there were little reminders of the season, and people we ran into provided connections to Christmas and the Christmas spirit. In Delhi one afternoon . . ."

Charlotte turned to nodding at Marilyn's sermonette and sipping—very gratefully sipping—her coffee and working on rising up into the world again. There wasn't anything she wanted more at this moment than to go back to bed—hopefully without the thumping of the night before—and let Marilyn and Brenda tackle the markets on their own. But another part of her—the strongest part at the moment—wanted to spend every moment she could of this vacation with Brenda. So, as long as the coffee supply didn't give out on this boat in the next half hour, she'd be putting on her game face and marching down the paths between the wooden booths in Nürnberg's center square along with Marilyn and Brenda—with Chance no doubt tagging behind with a game face of his own in place.

As the four were leaving the dining room, the two elderly ladies were also rising to leave, and Marilyn stopped to force introductions. Marilyn always knew everyone in the vicinity very soon after touching ground—and people gravitated to her with their problems, as well. In this regard, her calling to the ministry had been ideal.

Tall and thin's real name was Irene Summersdale, a retired librarian, who made quite clear that she was traveling as companion to short and stout Hattie Timmons, who identified herself only as a frequent traveler—which bowled over Charlotte a bit. How this woman had been reacting to the cruise so far had given Charlotte the feeling that it was her first—and most probably her last—cruise vacation ever.

"You were showing Hattie some lovely antique jewelry yesterday at the airport," Charlotte said, half way knowing that she was working her way into the center of the about-turn in Irene's mood from the previous day. And, indeed, Irene immediately looked downcast.

"Yes, but I have mislaid it somehow since then. We've . . . I've looked everywhere for it."

"Oh, dear," Marilyn said, taking Irene's hand, a gesture that seemed to have an immediate calming effect on the other woman. "We must look harder for them, then. After the outing today, perhaps we can put our heads together with you—Charlotte was a senior FBI investigator, you know. We'll just have to retrace your steps here in Nürnberg before the boat sails."

"Speaking of today's outing," Hattie interjected somewhat sourly, as she began maneuvering around the group by making legs move under the threat of her jabbing cane, "if I don't start moving toward the buses, you will have made me miss the shopping trip. And I've come here for a good nativity set."

With that, everyone started moving toward their cabins. At some point, Charlotte noticed that Marilyn was no longer wearing her jeweled Christmas tree brooch—but it only vaguely registered with her as Brenda was urging her into their cabin for final preparations for the trip and Chance was doing the same with Marilyn at their cabin door.

Fifteen minutes later, as Charlotte and Brenda were at the top of the gangplank, ready to descend and find their assigned bus, Charlotte saw that the Mercedes limousine she'd seen at the pier the previous day was back and that Sophia and Hans Eberhardt were standing at a passenger door being held open by a chauffeur. Another couple were entering the car and were inside before Charlotte had a chance to get a good look at them. She wondered who had already connected with the Eberhardts. She also thought of finding an Internet café while they were downtown and e-mailing the Annapolis FBI office to report an Eberhardt sighting, in case that might help their ongoing investigation. But then she thought that this might be taken as a move to connect with Evan Worthington, so she put it out of her mind.

Putting it out of her mind was easy at the moment, as the buses were showing signs of wanting to depart and Charlotte and Brenda were still trapped at the top of the gang plank. They had come off the ship behind the Japanese couple, who had stopped at the top of the gang plank, denying any movement around them, and were posing with their Cabbage Patch "child" for a photograph that they were having difficulty convincing the sailors on the pier to take for them.

Charlotte solved the problem by offering to take the photo herself and mumbling to Brenda to get to a bus and make sure it held for her.

* * * *

The four of them were at the center of Nürnberg Christmas market, following a satisfying meal of sausages, potato salad, and beer—which Chance insisted on verbalizing by the German spelling "*Bier*" in homage to actually being in Germany to drink it—when Charlotte got to use her first "aha, told you so" facial expression for Brenda.

They heard Chance's name being called out over the festive snowy scene before they had any idea who was calling out. "*Doktor Diamond! Wo ist Doktor Diamond, bitte!*"

Their tour guide was so disconcerted that he'd forgotten to call out in English rather than German. Luckily, there didn't seem to be a lot of other Doctor Diamonds at the Nürnberg Christmas fair that day, so Chance followed the voice—and Charlotte, Brenda, and Marilyn followed Chance.

"It's Mrs. Melard," Dietrich Hahn was telling Chance almost breathlessly, as the women caught up with the doctor. "I'm afraid she's had a fall. I've called for a bus to come as closely to where she is as possible—but she insists on going back to the boat. She says she doesn't want to be stuck in a German hospital after the boat has left Nürnberg. And you, I believe, are the only physician on the boat. Would you mind terribly taking a look at her and determining what we should do? We haven't moved her."

"Yes, of course, take us to her," Chance answered. "And my wife's a minister; she should be able to help lessen Mrs. Melard's stress."

The three of them, Dietrich, with Chance and Marilyn in tow, moved off at a quick pace, and Charlotte and Brenda followed them at a short distance.

"That look," Brenda said, turning to Charlotte.

"Yes, it's a 'told you so' look," Charlotte said.

"Nobody has died. At worst it's a broken leg."

"Give it time. The Chance Diamond curse is just starting to build up, I'm afraid. And with Marilyn added into the mix, we'll have a regular clinic and rehab facility going on board within a few days. We won't see them the rest of the cruise."

"Which is probably what you wanted all along," Brenda said with an amused laugh.

When they caught up with Chance, he was bending over and examining Doris Melard's ankle. Malcolm Melard was hovering nearby, and Rico had just driven up with one of the smaller buses. He could get within sight of them, but not all of the way to Mrs. Melard's side, where she had tripped off a curb at the edge of the city square where the wooden booths of the outdoor market were set up.

"I think it's just a sprain," Chance was saying.

"No local hospitals," Doris was mumbling. "The ship, please. Don't leave me here. One last vacation. I want this one last vacation. The Rhine castles."

"A word, Doctor Diamond, if I could," Professor Melard leaned down to Chance and murmured. They went off to the side,

42

leaving Marilyn to comfort Doris. Charlotte could see that the two men were deep in conversation, and that they eventually motioned Dietrich to join them. Dietrich flipped open his cell phone and made a short phone call. When the men came back to Doris, Chance said, "Your husband and Dietrich will help us get you moved to the bus, and we'll take you back to the boat. I think all I need do is wrap it and we'll see what we can come up with in the way of painkillers. Is that OK with you, Dietrich?"

The tour director didn't look too sure of himself, even after the conversation he'd had with Chance and Professor Melard and on the telephone, but Chance added, "I'll follow up with her on the cruise. If it appears to be something more serious than a sprain, we can get medical attention for her at one of the other stops."

Both Chance and Professor Melard were looking hard at Dietrich, who shrugged and said, "If it's only a sprain, and you'll take care of her, then, yes, that sounds like the best avenue to take." They could tell that he wasn't all that excited about all of the fuss and paperwork that would be involved in taking her to a hospital here. The boat was set to launch within a couple of hours of the end of this city tour.

"You ladies can continue shopping," Chance said. "I'll go back to the boat with the Melards on the bus."

"I'll go with you, certainly," Marilyn said, her calling trumping her need to shop—with Doris Melard giving her a look of appreciation—and Charlotte's signal to Brenda that she'd welcome this opportunity to trade shopping in the cold snow for the comforts of a nap in their suite was deftly caught, and the first outing at a Christmas market ended for all of them.

When they got back to the boat, Charlotte easily convinced Brenda that a "nap" was much more interesting and invigorating than another hour at the market.

* * * *

"How is she?"

"Mrs. Melard or Marilyn?" Chance asked. He'd sidled up to Charlotte and Brenda in the lounge during the official captain's welcome reception before dinner that evening. Charlotte was finding that, although a Tom Collins wasn't nearly as interesting as a Harvey Wallbanger, it tasted a bit better, while Brenda was being adventuresome this evening with the other special, a Blue Atlantic. Charlotte had passed that up, pointing out that she didn't trust it as they weren't actually on the Atlantic.

"And if we were, you'd be seasick," Brenda countered, with a laugh.

"Mrs. Melard." Charlotte answered Chance's question, pointedly ignoring Brenda's joke. "Are you saying there's something wrong with Marilyn too? Where is she?"

"She's tearing the cabin apart," Chance answered. "When we got back this afternoon, she couldn't find that brooch she was wearing at breakfast."

"Oh, I meant to mention that," Charlotte said. "I noticed that she wasn't wearing it when we returned to the cabins after breakfast. I suggest you try looking in the dining room."

"Well, I'll be off to do that," Chance said. "We'll see you in the dining room. I'm not much for receptions anyway. Pretty crowded in here. Oh, and Mrs. Melard is resting in her cabin. They had a nice selection of drugs in their sick room here. Pretty extensive for the purposes of a river cruise boat, I'd think."

Charlotte wanted to ask him what had transpired between him and Professor Melard—why the insistence that Doris Melard be brought back to the boat rather than to a clinic or hospital in Nürnberg, but Chance was gone before she could—and she knew that he probably wouldn't tell her anyway, considering it doctor-patient privilege.

Without even realizing it, Charlotte found that she and Brenda were standing in the reception line to shake hands with the captain—in fact, they seemed to be at the tail end of the line. Charlotte probably would have stepped out of line—reception queues being one of her least favorite activities—but she had decided that it was time to have a word with the captain.

He was younger than she would have thought and quite handsome. She'd seen his name and photo posted by the reception desk out in the main foyer, but he was even better looking in person than in the photo. She thought he must be Norwegian or from some other Scandinavian country. His name was Kurt Jorgenson.

She almost did pull Brenda out of line, though, when the captain was involved in an unusually long chat with two men several people ahead of them—and didn't seem at all interested in shortening the discussion. The older of the two, appearing to be in his late forties, was distinguished looking. He was leaning on a cane—and when he departed from the side of the captain, Charlotte saw that he had a decided limp. Perhaps, she thought, that was why she hadn't seen him in any of the groups at the Christmas market that afternoon. The man at his side was decidedly younger and was the sultry brooding type, with blond curls and long eyelashes, sensual lips, and, Charlotte thought, probably thinking a bit too much of himself and his irresistible charm.

But at last they were next in line, and Captain Jorgenson's face was lighting up. "Brenda Brandon, the actress. Surely it must be." His eyes were all for Brenda. Charlotte didn't mind. He was a bit too suave for her.

"Brenda Boynton. That's my real name," Brenda told him. "I'm on vacation from all of that other nonsense."

"But then you actually know David Runion, don't you . . . and Tony Trice. Great actors both. And such stage presence."

Brenda and Charlotte almost broke down in the giggles. It was Brenda's longtime movie partner that the captain was enchanted by. Not her.

"And this is my friend, Charlotte Diamond," Brenda said, pulling Charlotte forward.

"Ah, yes. Related to Doctor Diamond and his wife in Suite 1, I take it."

"Yes," Charlotte answered. "We seem to be the last in your line, and I would like to talk with you about something for a minute, please."

"I haven't met Doctor Diamond yet, I don't think," the captain continued on his own course. "Could you tell him for me how grateful I am that he has helped one of our other passengers this afternoon."

"Yes, certainly, Captain. But I think there's something else you should know."

"They're starting into dinner," Brenda interjected. "I'll just go ahead to the dining room and I'll find Chance and Marilyn."

"Yes, fine," Charlotte said. She turned toward the captain and his quizzical look.

* * * *

"Well, I'll be. How interesting," Charlotte said fifteen minutes later, after she had navigated the glad handing of Pierre, the obsequious maitre d', and as she and Brenda and the Diamonds were looking over the menu for the evening.

"What, you can't choose between the beef tenderloin and the roasted vegetables in filo?" Brenda asked.

"Not that—although it's no contest. The beef, of course—and maybe both the fruit mousse and cheese plate for desert. No, our cruise has just been augmented from the top drawer."

The other three looked up at that, in time to follow the entrance of Sophia and Hans Eberhardt into the dining room, with

Pierre strutting along in front of them, obviously very much aware of who he had in tow. Following them was a couple neither Charlotte nor Brenda had seen on the boat before. The woman was a good six foot two and just this side of hefty. She would be called zaftig in art and model circles, probably, but she carried it well, although Charlotte couldn't quite understand why she wasn't falling over in trying to keep her posture. She knew this was rather catty of her, though, because the woman's posture was perfect—majestic even. It wasn't just her bosoms that were challenging her balance. She was dripping in diamonds. She perhaps was on the dark side of forty, but there obviously had been an army of groomers taking care of her. The man with her was a good ten years younger than she was. He was quite good looking, but in a swarthy, dangerous gangsterish way. The way he moved in relationship to the woman left no doubt she was in charge and he had been bought. Assuming this was so, though, Charlotte didn't thing he'd come cheaply.

The two couples headed for tables in opposite directions, but just seeing them together made Charlotte realize that the newly observed couple were the ones who had been getting in Hans Eberhardt's limousine earlier in the day.

"Candace Harrington," Charlotte said sotto voce, not wanting to be overheard by the new couple moving past them to a table that had a reserved sign on it at the back corner of the restaurant, with windows to both port and aft, which would give them two great views of the ship launching and moving into the river channel, as it was then doing.

"Candace Harrington?" Marilyn said somewhat louder, although, happily, the couple had passed them by at that point. "The heiress who was kidnapped."

"The same. Some time ago, of course."

"Something to do with revolutionaries, wasn't it?" Chance asked.

"Yes," Charlotte answered. "Her father was probably the largest arms manufacturer in the country, and she was kidnapped and held for months—with the ransom being that her father divest himself completely."

"Which he didn't do, as I recall."

"No. He said publicly that they could have her—that she was costing him too much anyway. He was actually cooperating with us—with the FBI—in not acceding to any of their demands, but the country didn't seem to react well to his apparent uncaring bravado in turning them down. We weren't sure subsequently that Candace appreciated it much either when she was released. I understand that father and daughter were estranged from that point and, whereas she'd been the good and dutiful daughter before the kidnapping, she turned into quite a hellion afterward. He's dead some five years and now she's running his armaments business."

"Rather a bloody rescue, as I remember," Chance said.

"Yes," Charlotte confirmed. "The father was said to have paid off some local police once we'd tracked down where they were holding her, and they went in and wiped them all out in a gun battle. She was wounded—an arm wound I think, which is probably why she's wearing that dress she is tonight—so the scars don't show. There

49

have been case studies claiming to show that her complete change in behavior was a reaction to her traumatic experience. She's certainly referred to as a rich bitch in most circles now. And she's known as a ruthless businesswoman."

"And 'rich bitch' is how I will dub her," Chance said, with a little laugh. "Interesting that she's on this cruise."

"I wouldn't suggest calling her that within her earshot. I understand that she travels most of the time now," Charlotte answered. "But I would imagine that she would be quite paranoid about her safety—there was a second attempt to kidnap her shortly after her father died that was only narrowly averted, and the business came under her leadership without missing a beat. The kidnappers didn't survive the attempt."

Having said that, Charlotte's professional instincts set in and her eyes traveled around the room. Was it her imagination—or the power of suggestion from their conversation—that she imagined she saw three men in the dining room she hadn't seen before who looked more like thugs than vacationers and who had their eyes glued to one of the tables the Eberhardts or Candace Harrington had gone to. Two young men were sitting together near the Eberhardt table, and a third, more dangerous looking than the other two, was sitting near Charlotte's table at the far corner from the Harrington table but showing close attention to Candace Harrington's every move.

"Oh, look," Marilyn said. "We're moving, and we're already out in the channel."

"Let's raise our glasses," Chance said, lifting his wine glass toward the middle of the table to be instantly joined by three more. "Off on an adventure."

"For better or worse," Charlotte muttered.

"Oh, Charlotte," Brenda responded. "Don't assume the worst." She was laughing her tinkling laugh, though, so the wine was already having its effect in keeping the party spirit alive. The two Tom Collinses Charlotte drank at the captain's reception didn't hurt either.

Marilyn hadn't found her brooch yet, and a brief look of pain flashed across her face when Charlotte mentioned "for worse," but she was of the optimistic variety and assumed the brooch would turn up eventually—and had decided not to let worry about it spoil her vacation until it did show up.

* * * *

Late that night, being unable to sleep because of the thumping of the previous night that had assaulted their repose again, Charlotte got up, wrapped a robe about her, and padded out into the corridor and to the darkened lounge at the bow of the boat. She thought maybe watching the ship glide down the river passage would mesmerize her into sleep. The thumping was quite annoying. It only happened at night, it seemed—at least they hadn't heard it any other time they'd been in the cabin as yet—and it was intermittent. It had happened twice thus far this night but there was no discernible pattern of what brought it on or how long it lasted.

When she entered the lounge, she saw that she wasn't alone. The two men she'd seen talking at length with Captain Jorgenson at the reception were there, sitting in tub chairs right up at the bow of the boat. They hadn't noticed her, but Charlotte could clearly see that they were holding hands, so she moved off to a far corner of the lounge, deep in the shadows. She stared out toward the bank of the river, with its occasional village scenes, and concentrated on invoking numbing boredom.

That was hard to do with the murmuring she heard from the two men. They were far away enough and speaking softly enough that Charlotte couldn't hear what they were saying—but she almost could, which made her strain to be able to hear them, albeit involuntarily. The older man seemed to be snuffling and crying, and the younger man appeared to be trying to comfort him. Charlotte thought of trying to withdraw without bringing attention to herself, but as she started to rise from the tub chair she had wedged herself in, another figure entered the lounge.

He was tall and dressed in a white uniform that made his figure stand out in the dim light. Captain Jorgenson moved over to the other two men and squatted down between them and joined in the murmuring.

Charlotte felt trapped, which wasn't helping to make her sleepy. But thankfully this didn't last long. Abruptly, all three men stood and moved toward the entrance of the lounge, the two younger men moving slowly to permit the limping older man to keep up with them. When they were out of the lounge, Charlotte got up, intending to return to her cabin when the men had moved elsewhere. When she got to the entrance from the reception foyer into the lounge, Charlotte saw the blond head of the captain down in the stair well to the next deck below, and she was drawn over to the well. Looking down, she could see that the men had stopped at the first door on the left in the corridor leading aft in the foyer below. The younger man opened the door to that cabin, and all three men entered it and closed the door behind them.

Charlotte had the notion that maybe they'd go to the suite between hers and Chance's. But then, she thought, of course they hadn't. She just hadn't been thinking on all cylinders. Unless there was an even better suite hidden someplace on this ship, that cabin, of course, was where Candace Harrington and her boy toy were booked.

Charlotte sighed and walked silently down the corridor and to her own suite. So focused was she on not alerting anyone that she was in the corridor that she didn't notice the figure standing next to the reception desk in the foyer and watching her inch her way down the corridor. If she'd seen the more dangerous-looking of the thugs she'd observed earlier in the dining room watching her move—closely watching her but somewhat amused at the spectacle she was making of herself in her robe-clad, large-bodied, crouched-stealth down the corridor—Charlotte would have been embarrassed, if not overly surprised.

Brenda was asleep when Charlotte entered the cabin and, mercifully, there was no thumping noise. Even if there was more thumping to come, Charlotte was reasonably sure she could sleep through it. And if there was during the rest of that night, Charlotte didn't know it. She slept the sleep of the dead.

Chapter Four: Day Three: Bamberg

"I think I've discovered—"

"The mystery of the bumps in the night," Charlotte broke in, finishing her sister-in-law's sentence. They were up for an early breakfast. The *Rhine Maiden* had been gently motoring down the Main toward the Rhine all night at a pace that even Charlotte couldn't complain about and now was tied up at a pier near the town of Bamberg in the heart of Bavaria. They were only here for the morning, and this was both one of the most picturesque towns in Germany and one of the last opportunities to shop at a large, outdoor Christmas market before they started breaking them down. The next day was Christmas Eve, when, after a brief flurry of last-minute Christmas preparations, the country would essentially shut down for two days.

"Yes," Marilyn said. "But how on earth could you know what I'm talking about—or what I think I've discovered?"

"Just your blushing alone tells me I'm right, dear sister-in-law," Charlotte answered with a smug little smile on her lips. "And I don't think we need worry about that anymore. I had a word with the steward before we came to breakfast, and I trust that adjustments will be made while we are all touring Bamberg."

"Are you two going to stop talking in riddles and tell us what this is about?" Chance interjected.

"Tell him," Charlotte said, maintaining her little smile.

"No, please, you do it, Charlotte," Marilyn responded. "I admit that I blush at just the thought."

"Oh, I'll tell him," Brenda broke in.

"You?" Charlotte asked, suddenly taken down a notch in smugness.

"Of course," Brenda answering. "I've known from the first sound of the thumping. Remember, I am a child of Hollywood."

"Oh, very well, you can do the honors," Charlotte said, deflated a bit.

"Will someone tell me? Am I the only one who doesn't know?" Chance muttered in exasperation.

This was answered by "yeses" from three female voices in harmony, accompanied by twinkling laughter.

"The bumps in the night are from whatever couple is in the suite between ours, Chance," said Brenda. "They are being, what shall I say, very amorous—very often."

"That would be Candace Harrington and the latest gigolo she has in tow," Charlotte said. "I deduced that last night, and a check with the steward this morning confirmed my surmise. But he understood what I was requesting almost immediately and assured me that they have soft bolsters they can use to muffle the impact of the headboard on the wall. He said they'd put those behind the bed's headboard as soon as the couple left the cabin. I told him that might be almost never, and we both had a good laugh over that."

"Oh," Chance answered in a small voice, and it appeared that he was blushing now—not so much about what the thumping was about as that his three female compatriots had figured it out and he hadn't. He looked at his watch as a distraction and, seeing the time, said, "It's about time to go, ladies. We don't want to be late for the gathering for the tour."

Then he said "oh" again but in a much more forceful manner. And he now was staring beyond his table companions toward a table across the dining room.

Hearing the catch in his voice, all three women swiveled their faces toward him. Chance muttered the word "catatonia," and then all three women swiveled their faces toward where he was looking.

Charlotte's first thought when she looked across the dining room was "nativity scene," which she later thought was a little bizarre other than the focus on the fast-approaching Christmas and all this talk about Christmas markets. People had arisen from nearby tables and were gathered around the table where Doris and Malcolm Melard had been sitting. Doris was sitting in her chair, her sprained ankle raised onto the seat of another chair, looking rigidly across the room. Malcolm was standing over her, leaning down toward his wife's stiff form and whispering something. The dining room host, Pierre—who apparently did occasionally put in a morning appearance—was crouching over her from the other side, fanning her face—with no effect—with a stack of menus.

As Chance, followed by Marilyn, launched himself toward the Melard's table, Charlotte took a sharp look at where Doris was staring. The angle led her to the table where the Eberhardt's were dining and where the Swiss banker, Hans, his hand suspended in the air and holding a slice of buttered toast, was staring back at Doris, a little frown on his face. His wife, Sophia, sitting so that her side was toward the nonaction at the Melard table, was animatedly jabbering about something without noticing that her husband's attention was drawn elsewhere.

Charlotte's eyes scanned the room, her highly developed powers of observation, kicking in. Nearly everyone she'd focused on in the early days of the cruise was there. The elderly ladies were at a table near the Eberhardts, and Irene Summersdale, the tall, thin one, had risen and was moving toward the Melard's table. Hattie Timmons, dressed like she was going on safari, remained at the table, sour expression on her face, and holding a forkful of omelet she evidently didn't approve of for the waitress, Gretchen, to examine.

The Japanese couple, and their Cabbage Patch doll, were at a table between Charlotte's and the Melards', their complete attention focused on the doll—so much so that Chance had to ask the Japanese man to move the doll's chair in so that he had passage to Doris Melard. The two thug-like men who stuck out like sore thumbs in a vacation ensemble were there, in the corner, watching what was proceeding. The third, older man who Charlotte thought didn't belong here wasn't there. Neither were Candace Harrington and her young man—but their failure to arrive early for breakfast was explainable by the thumping in the night mystery that had already been solved.

Even Captain Jorgenson was there now, approaching through the entrance to the restaurant, the waiter Rico at his side, who undoubtedly had gone to fetch the captain as soon as the commotion had started. The captain stopped in the doorway, surveying the scene, but Rico moved in toward the Melards' table and Chance had to brush him aside too to get to Doris's side. Once there, Chance squatted down and began to examine Doris. She remained in her stiff trance, however. Marilyn also squatted down and took Doris's hand in hers, and, at that, Charlotte discerned a bit of flutter in Doris's eyelids.

"Please, everyone, stand back," Chance said in a calm voice. "Go back to your tables, please. She's having a bit of a seizure. We just need to take her to her cabin, and I think there's something I can give her to relieve this. Please, Pierre, please stop with the fanning. Someone, please, help move Pierre away. Please."

The dining room broke its tableau and started to return to normal, as Malcolm Melard, Rico, and a man from another table helped gently carry Doris toward their suite. Chance and Marilyn were at the entrance of the restaurant, conversing with the captain, and then Marilyn moved back to the table while Chance and the captain left the restaurant.

"Chance says he saw some Lorazepram in the drugs cabinet in the sick room when he was in there yesterday," Marilyn informed them. "He thinks a shot of that will bring her out of her trance. I'll sit with her while he's doing that and, with luck, we'll meet you in the lounge during the briefing before this morning's tour." Then she was gone again.

Charlotte looked around the dining room again as she finished her coffee and noted that life had returned almost to normal, although she was sure that everyone at the tables were discussing what had just transpired, giving it their own spin, and dredging up similar stories from their past. The Eberhardts had risen from their table and were moving toward the restaurant's entrance, and, out of the corner of her eye, Charlotte noted that the two young men who didn't fit rose almost simultaneously with the Eberhardts, and, when the Eberhardts had departed the restaurant, started to make their own move toward the door.

Were these policemen or young detectives, Charlotte wondered. Were Hans Eberhardt's movements being monitored by the authorities? If so, by the authorities of what country and was this not really a vacation for him? Was he up to something criminal? She laughed to herself on that. Every breath Hans Eberhardt took amounted to being up to something criminal.

When Charlotte and Brenda returned to their suite, Charlotte went immediately to the window and looked out onto the pier. Not a limousine this time, but a sleek Mercedes nonetheless. And she saw the car just in time to spy Hans Eberhardt getting into the backseat before the Mercedes glided away from the pier. Charlotte definitely decided that she needed to find an Internet café here in Bamberg and check in with the Annapolis FBI office—she knew that the presence of Eberhardt would have her on edge the entire cruise if she didn't check on what he might be doing here.

* * * *

Charlotte and Brenda entered the lounge in a babble of conversation. Many of those present had picked Brenda out as a movie actress of considerable fame already, so there was somewhat of a parting of the sea in front of them as they moved into the lounge and an interruption of conversations around them.

Charlotte had her antenna up, however, and she caught snatches of conversation as they walked, much of it concerning Doris Melard's catatonic trance in the restaurant just fifteen minutes earlier, but some other tidbits also that Charlotte honed in on.

"Just as lovely as in *The Spring of Mrs. Jensen*."

"And just staring there; it was really weird."

"I'm sure I brought it on the trip. I can't imagine what happened to it."

"White as a porcelain doll. And so delicate. I wonder why she even . . ."

"He'll be out in a moment. A little delicate this morning. His heart, you know . . ."

This last murmuring caught Charlotte's attention, and she turned to see that it had been spoken by the young, blond Byronish type who had been speaking so long with the captain along with the distinguish looking older gentleman—the younger one Chance had, in fact nicknamed Lord B. and the older man who had been with him O.W. for reasons he wouldn't tell Charlotte. The young man was talking with Irene Summersdale, who evidently had asked about the older gentleman.

Charlotte heard Hattie Timmons snort, "Well, he'd better get a move on if he wants to be on the tour. We're already running late. Typical."

Charlotte and Brenda moved on to where two tub chairs at a table by the dance floor miraculously opened up for them. Charlotte knew that no one had cleared space for her—that she hadn't been seen by anyone in the lounge. All eyes were on Brenda. Soon after they sat, first Marilyn, and then Chance, dragged up two more tub chairs and joined them.

"Is Doris settled?" Brenda asked. "But more important, I guess, is she conscious?"

"Yes, she's awake now and is just weak. She's calm. The Lorazepram worked, but . . ."

He stopped there, shutting his mouth like it was a steel trap door.

"But what, Chance?" Charlotte honed in on him. She could see that he was quite concerned about something.

"It isn't about Mrs. Melard or her condition. There should be enough medicine for her—at least until the ship's stores can be replenished."

"Replenished?" Charlotte asked. "Yesterday you were saying that the cruise ship was a veritable floating pharmacy—much better stocked than you thought it would be."

"Yes, well, since yesterday someone has nearly cleared out the drug supply. We were lucky that they didn't take the Lorazepram. They seemed to know what was readily marketable and what wasn't."

"Drugs have been stolen?" The question was from Marilyn. Her eyes had gone wide.

Charlotte wasn't nearly as surprised. "The country shuts down for a couple of days tomorrow. You sure you have enough to treat Doris Melard?"

"Yes, of Lorazepram. There may be other drugs we need, but we'll just have to make do. The captain said he'd contact the cruise line office and try to have some new supplies ready to pick up tomorrow when we dock at Würzburg. And, of course, there will have to be an investigation. I'm sure there's been a theft."

Charlotte turned and gave Brenda a sharp look, and the movie star, in turn, whispered, "I know what you're thinking. But no one has died yet. It isn't the family curse."

"Not yet, but just wait," Charlotte murmured back. But then she turned to Chance and said in a louder voice, "Do you think Doris will make it to the end of the cruise?"

Chance just shrugged.

"She's on her last legs, isn't she? That's why she didn't want to go to the hospital in Nürnberg. I heard her say she wanted this last trip."

"I don't think it's that alarming. She's unwell, yes, but there's nothing immediately endangering her life. If she were my patient, I'd have some tests run on her. It appears to be something lingering, but . . ."

"But what?" Charlotte asked.

"I've already said too much, I'm afraid, Charlotte. You know I can't . . ."

"I guess you don't have to. It would be quite a news splash if she were to die on this cruise. I believe she's worth well over a hundred million dollars. I wouldn't have thought there was enough mustard in the world to add up to that—but I guess the Pease family is into other condiments too."

Chance started to respond, but there was a drum roll from the sound system and Dietrich Hahn was standing on the small dance floor and starting to give instructions for the day's trip to Bamberg. During his briefing, he very clearly noted that there were two choices, based on how strenuous the guests wanted the experience to be. There would be a lot of walking, much of it uphill on cobblestone streets for one group, but those not feeling up to that would have a small bus take them from location to location. They would see the same sights; they just wouldn't be walking the streets between them.

The ones taking the easier of the two tours were asked to go to the dock first. Charlotte and her friends were dismayed when they saw that, although Irene Summersdale rose and joined the first tour group, which also included the elder gentleman Chance called O.W. and the younger Lord B., Hattie Timmons stayed put for the more difficult walk. Considering her size, age, and that she walked with a cane and wheezed whenever she looked at a set of stairs, Charlotte's assumption—and she could see in watching his face, Dietrich Hahn's hope—had been that Hattie would be taking the easier tour.

As would be the perpetual fate of Charlotte's foursome, the Japanese couple wound up in the same small group—which was led by a slender young woman named Fraulein Miessen—with Charlotte's quartet. Malcolm Melard hadn't come to the lounge, presumably choosing to spend the day with his wife, and of course Candace Harrington and her young man weren't up yet. The Eberhardts had already left for somewhere in a private car. The older of the thug-like men Charlotte was worried about was in the lounge, drinking coffee and reading a newspaper, during Hahn's briefing, but he made no move to leave for the tour.

"And, so, here's to Bamberg," Brenda said, as she stood up. "To Shopping."

"To Medieval architecture," said Chance.

"To enduring it," croaked Charlotte.

"To the cathedral," pronounced Marilyn. All stared at her. "Well, it can't all be shopping," answered Marilyn as they headed for the gang plank. "And I've heard they have a gorgeous cathedral here."

The quartet found that Bamberg did, indeed have a lovely cathedral, the cathedral and Benedictine abbey of Michaelsberg in the Baroque style, which was located high above the town on the original site of the eleventh-century castle of the royal house of Badenberg. And the walk up from the central square, where they were let off and where they were instructed to return to for a short buying spree in the Christmas market, rose through a picturesque town that had been spared the devastation of World War II. But it really rose to that site, via narrow cobblestoned streets, and the going was ponderous because Hattie Timmons huffed and puffed and cursed and swore the whole way and eventually had to be almost picked up between two of the men in the party and carried along—which she didn't appreciate one bit either.

The main attraction at the cathedral—beyond just standing on the lofty expansive platform it was built on and looking out over Bamberg and the surrounding countryside—was the carved altar screen in one of its chapels. The groups were led in there and stood in awe, picking out the tableaus and individual saint's stories that were worked into the intricate carving on the back wall, splashed with light from the clerestory windows.

Charlotte and her colleagues were immediately struck with wonder at this sight, which was accompanied by the recorded sounds of an ethereal-sounding boys' choir. But Charlotte, like the rest in the chapel at the time, were a lot less in awe of the Japanese couple that was with them. The woman had picked this time and place to decide that their Cabbage Patch baby needed to have its diaper changed, and she proceeded to do that in a center pew, while cooing and baby talking to the rag doll—presumably in Japanese. As she was doing so, her husband moved around the periphery of the group that was spending as much time and effort watching this strange event on the pew as they were using their limited time to admire the carved altar screen. The Japanese man had a camera—and was snapping photographs, although photography, of course, was forbidden in this chapel. But the oddness of how he was going about this, leaning against this person or that—people who were watching the diaper-changing ritual—and cajoling others to get into the shot he was taking, seemed quite invasive and prevented any religious feeling of being in the chapel. It was odd enough that Charlotte started watching him, rather than anything else, and became perplexed. She wanted to know more about this Japanese couple now.

And her perplexity was added to as they were struggling down from the monastery mount to the Christmas market below, because when they got close to the market, she caught a glimpse of their boat captain and the O.W. and Lord B. duo entering another of the narrow streets leading up from the city center. Quite a cozy crew that, she was thinking.

She accompanied the Diamonds and Brenda to the edge of the market but then begged off the shopping spree there, saying she needed to find an Internet café because she needed to check in on some people back in the States, including checking on how their dogs, Sam and Rocket, were doing. She opined that they no doubt were being grossly spoiled by the young woman, Sherry Landon, who was renting the house next door to Charlotte's house in Hopewell. And, oh yeah, she had to check with the Realtor trying to rent or sell Charlotte's house because Charlotte had moved in with Brenda.

Charlotte looked at her watch. "What time should we meet back here—I presume this is the place we should meet for the bus?"

"Yep, this is the place," Chance answered. "The schedule said the last bus would leave at 12:30. So, I'd say we should be here no later than 12:20. Let's synchronize our . . . hmmmm."

"What is it, hon?" said Marilyn.

"I seem to have left my watch back on the boat," Chance said. "I'm not wearing it. Strange."

"Strange indeed," Charlotte thought, not so sure Chance had left his watch anywhere. Jewelry was having a habit of being misplaced on this cruise. She knew he'd had the watch on at breakfast. This was developing into something a little sticky-fingered—and it was hitting close to home now. This was getting personal. Although Marilyn hadn't mentioned that her Christmas brooch was still missing, she hadn't said she'd found it either.

Charlotte had other things she wanted to check on the Internet now as much, if not more than, the topics she had ticked off to Chance and the women. As she was walking off, she saw that the Japanese couple was already beginning to tank up on Christmas delights in the market and that Candace Harrington and her companion had finally surfaced, and she was doing a lot of buying too. On a less happy note, the older of the thug-like men from the tour boat had decided to come into town after all, and seemed to be walking aimlessly around. But he was actually following Harrington around at some distance. Charlotte wasn't fooled. She knew what surveillance looked like.

At the Internet café, she e-mailed her former assistant at the FBI Annapolis office, Margaret Fancel, reporting not only the presence of Hans Eberhardt and wondering if he was under official surveillance but also asking for some other background information. She wanted to know if there had been any indications lately that Candace Harrington was being set up for another kidnapping attempt or whether she was involved in anything that would bring her under official surveillance. While she was there, not having used up her full hour after sending e-mails to Hopewell, Charlotte did some searching on the Internet.

Fifteen minutes later, cutting it close now to be at the bus back to the boat on time, Charlotte whistled as she stood up. "Very interesting. The rumor mill reports that Doris Melard was looking for

67

her next husband already. I wonder if Malcolm Melard is aware of that. I'm sure he finds her millions quite comforting."

Chapter Five: Still Day Three: En Route to Würzburg: Captain's Dinner

The captain's festive welcoming dinner was preceded that evening by a briefing in the lounge on what lay ahead for Christmas Eve after the boat docked at Würzburg the next morning. They weren't staying in that city for the entire day, despite its many historical sites, including the Residenz, the Prince Bishop Palace that was considered one of Europe's greatest palaces, or the Medieval fortress of Mariensburg floating over the city. It was Christmas Eve and Germany was closing down. Some of the high-tourist areas in the region were still open, though, and the day's escorted tour was by bus to Rothenburg ob der Tauber, which was one of the best-preserved examples of a Medieval walled town in Germany, not having been destroyed in any part since the Thirty Years War in the early seventeenth century.

This, Dietrich Hahn also noted—to groans rolling around the lounge, including from Marilyn and Brenda—would effectively be the last open Christmas market for them to visit.

"Better decide on those purchases you are mulling but haven't bought yet," he said. "And don't worry about size. You will have opportunities to mail all of your prizes home in time to be there when you arrive. Of course we will have vendors coming aboard to offer unique wares over the next week as well."

Marilyn visibly perked up at hearing this information.

For once, nearly all of the ship's guests appeared to be present in the lounge, most likely in high-energy anticipation of the captain's dinner about to begin in the Lorelei restaurant. The Eberhardts were there and even Candace Harrington and her escort were present. Candace was dripping in diamonds again and was standing center stage on the dance floor, giving the overhead spotlights every opportunity to pick up and transmit the sparkle of them around the room. The younger man with her was also handsomely decked out in a tuxedo. In looks he rivaled the friend of the older man with the cane—the young man Chance had termed Lord B., and Lord B., who had been in the spotlight before Candace Harrington and escort made their grand appearance, had now slunk into the shadows in the presence of such a rival in young male beauty.

Still, Lord B. hadn't completely retreated; he was sticking very close to the older man—termed O.W. by Chance—and fussing over him in a way that the older man obviously found unnecessary and a bit annoying.

As much in the limelight as Candace Harrington was standing, though, Charlotte was proud to see that it was Brenda who was getting most of the attention and appreciative looks. She didn't need either diamonds or a spotlight. She brought her own luminance and charisma.

At the sound of a gong, Pierre Pelletier, the maitre d', appeared at the entrance of the lounge, looking like a nervous thoroughbred racehorse chomping at the bit to burst out of the gate at the races. Raising a microphone to his lips, he asked that the guests he named be the first to enter the restaurant, along with their escorts, and to proceed to the captain's table, set up in the center of the Lorelei. Charlotte was not surprised when she heard Candace Harrington's name and that of Hans Eberhardt, but when she heard her own name—and those of Brenda, Chance, and Marilyn—she initially was a little shocked. She hadn't considered at all who would be invited to the captain's table. When the next names called out were Japanese—if ruptured Japanese in Pierre's nervous pronunciation—and the couple with the Cabbage Patch doll stood up as Charlotte's party passed them, Charlotte realized that Pierre was just running down the list of those booked in the first-class suites.

Once they got to the table and started looking for their individual name card, though, the mystery that Charlotte had solved reopened. There were eighteen places set and, at Charlotte's count, only twelve passengers in the first-class cabins. Candace Harrington and her escort, who was shortly introduced as Felix Satoris—with no occupation identified—and Sophia and Hans Eberhardt were already seated by the time Charlotte and her party arrived. Then Malcolm Melard, who Charlotte hadn't seen in the lounge even though she had been keen on locating him, magically materialized, giving regrets for his wife—regrets that obviously already were anticipated as there was no place set for her. To Charlotte's chagrin, the Japanese husband and wife were placed next to her, with the woman introducing herself as Mary Hamata and her husband as Jack Hamata as they were sitting down. They placed the Cabbage Patch doll in a chair between them that Charlotte could hardly believe had been allotted to the rag doll by the Lorelei staff. Charlotte was forced to express interest when Mary Hamata, with a serious face, introduced the doll as her daughter, Akachan. Brenda was later to inform her, with a laugh, that *akachan* simply meant "baby" in Japanese.

The captain and Dietrich Hahn appeared, solving Charlotte's seating shortfall by two more chairs, although the lack of a chair for Delores Melard discounted that to one.

To Charlotte's amusement, and Candace Harrington's obvious chagrin, Brenda had been seated on the captain's right. But, as Candace was seated directly across from the captain at the oblong table, he could always say that she was given precedence in terms of conversation. The guest seated at the captain's left was a surprise to Charlotte—and solved part of the mystery—but it was only an initial surprise. The distinguished elder O.W., quickly revealed to be a novelist by the name of Bernard—who his friend called Bernie—Colson. The young man with him was introduced as Sean Richards.

"Uh," Richards hesitated a long moment before answering when asked his profession. "Book editor?" was what he came up with—more in the form of a question than a statement.

"Sean does read my manuscripts for me," Bernard Colson said, with a slight jab in his tone, "and I find his critique's quite helpful—and surprising, considering that he was cleaning my pool when we first met."

Charlotte made a mental note to check out what sort of books Colson wrote when she had a chance to get back on the Internet at their next landing. The look on young Richards' face was, she thought, priceless when Colson cut his legs out from underneath him. She appreciated an acerbic wit like that, and perhaps would enjoy his writing. She stole a quick glance over at Candace's boy toy, Felix Satoris, who looked equally insulted and put in his place. It would be very amusing, Charlotte thought, if he had once been Candace Harrington's pool boy as well.

If Charlotte was initially surprised by the seating of the novelist and his companion, she quickly decided it shouldn't be surprising in view of the two times she had seen the captain with them. She wondered if there perhaps was some family connection, but Captain Jorgenson was quite pronouncedly Scandinavian, and the other two men weren't.

Then she received a genuine, out-of-the-blue, surprise as Pierre helped Irene Summersdale and Hattie Timmons to the last two vacant chairs.

"Miss Timmons is an especially honored guest," Captain Jorgenson said, as he motioned the other guests to sit, while he and Dietrich Hahn remained standing. "She has the record on this cruise for the number of cruises she's taken with our line. This is, if I've counted correctly, her thirty-second cruise."

"Thirty-fourth," Hattie Timmons corrected him sourly as she shot Rico a look of censure for having pulled Irene's chair out before hers.

"Thirty-four?" Charlotte thought. "Is the woman a masochist for putting herself through ordeals she quite clearly doesn't enjoy—or a sadist for enjoying putting the staffs of cruise lines and the passengers through ordeals? Perhaps she can't stand the thought of anyone else enjoying herself."

She found she was starting to say something, but then Brenda was putting her hand on her arm. Charlotte looked up and saw that Brenda too, was amused, but that it was probably just too funny for words—that it was quite possible that the Timmons woman wouldn't appreciate the joke.

Charlotte had wondered who they were going to seat in the eighteen chairs, but then she could see that the problem was that there weren't enough chairs. A mountain of a man all dressed in white and with a chef's hat on was standing, looking perplexed, behind the seat now occupied by the Hamatas' "baby," Akachan. The Hamatas weren't showing any sign of giving the chair up to him, even though the name tag at the seating quite clearly was his. He had even reached over and picked the place card up to establish that it identified him. After a minute, Charlotte remembered that he was the head chef Chance had nicknamed Hardy when seen standing beside the maitre d' he'd nicknamed Laurel. The issue was resolved when, at a snap of the fingers from the captain, Rico was set in motion to pull up another chair and for Gretchen to quickly set another place setting. The man then was introduced as Chef Horst, who would discuss the foods and wines being served to the captain's table that evening.

Everyone seated and having chosen between the sirloin of venison or halibut "en Pappilotte," the captain started around the table in more formal introductions.

"Just a simple banker," Hans Eberhardt said. "I just live in the shadow of my wife, Sophia. She's a TV actress in Italy, you know? Her English is not too good, and it embarrasses her, so I will speak for her."

Apparently no one—except for Brenda, of course, and also Felix Satoris, who salivated a bit over the information that Sophia was an Italian film star to the marked chagrin of Candace Harrington—had known that, but the way Sophia was ready to burst out of her décolletage alone was enough to convince them all.

Charlotte nearly gagged on her wine when Eberhardt said he was a simple banker and he looked up hard at her, with eyes flashing, but he quickly got control of himself and subsided into studied dulldom.

As far as speaking for his wife, Charlotte thought, "I just bet you don't want her talking to anyone about anything. She might reveal what you are up to. You're always up to something."

No one pursued Irene Summersdale's former profession beyond the librarian identification, although in the lounge after dinner, Charlotte learned that Irene's library had been at the FBI training and research facilities in Quantico, Virginia, and the two had a lively discussion about legendary agents they both had known and the type of data Irene worked with. Hattie wouldn't own up to any profession other than professional traveler.

Chance snickered and Marilyn had to stomp on his foot under the table when Felix Satoris said that he was a race jockey. Marilyn immediately turned and gave Charlotte a warning look when her sister-in-law muttered something about riding old nags, but, although Candace looked up sharply at the snicker, she didn't seem to have heard what Charlotte whispered.

The Hamatas were into pharmaceuticals, Jack Hamata claimed, and Charlotte knew that there, indeed, was a major Japanese pharmaceutical corporation by that name. Chance had muttered something to her about that as soon as he'd heard the name "Hamata" spoken by the wife in her informal introductions with Charlotte. During the appetizer course, Chance tried to engage Jack in a discussion of the various new drugs the Hamata corporation was turning out, but Jack had a hard time following Chance's English, he said, and half way into the main course, he declared that it was Akachan's bedtime and that he'd be back after putting the baby to bed.

Malcolm Melard left the table at the same time, having asked Gretchen to wrap up his own meal and something to take to Doris—that he didn't think he should leave her alone for very long. Rico was no longer in evidence at this point, having been replaced by another waiter Charlotte hadn't met yet.

Everyone already had reason to know that Chance was a physician, although they all seemed to look more closely with surprise when Marilyn told them, rather reluctantly, that she was a minister. As she was afraid, they all seemed a bit more reserved in the language they used during the remainder of the meal. And everyone, of course, also knew that Brenda was a movie star—or had been, she declared. When several of them voiced disappointment at her statement that she was retired, Charlotte piped up and said, "I don't think Brenda will ever retire. She'll be filming down in Florida later this spring."

"And you, Miss Diamond," Bernie Colson asked, "do you have a profession? I take it you and Dr. Diamond are related?"

"Yes, he's my brother. My older brother," Charlotte said, a twinkle in her eye at having gotten that in before Candace could ask if she was Chance's mother. She said nothing further, not caring if everyone thought she was his spinster sister, traveling on his nickel.

"Charlotte's a famous detective," Brenda interjected. "She was a senior FBI investigator, the pride of their Annapolis office, before I stole her away and made her mine."

This caused faces to jerk up, to be sure—most because of Brenda's bald claim of her relationship with Charlotte—but a few, Charlotte could see, more obviously at the mention of the FBI. Charlotte looked directly at Hans Eberhardt for his response, which was all she could have hoped for. He almost sank under the table. But she also noted, in her peripheral vision, reactions from Felix Satoris, Sean Richards, the captain—and even, surprisingly, from Mary Hamatas. Charlotte decided she'd have a busy time perusing the Internet and checking names and backgrounds the next time she could get at it.

"But what about you, Captain Jorgenson?" Brenda asked, clearing the tension from the air by turning to their host. "I would think that the life on a cruise ship on the European rivers would be an exciting and demanding job. Do you have family—a wife and children—and are you able to be with them often?"

Chance snickered again under his breath, but only Marilyn and Charlotte heard that, Charlotte thought. Marilyn's face was wrapped in confusion.

"I'm afraid there's little room for a family on river cruise boats," the captain answered. "The staff of the boat are my family. The boat is my wife; the river is my mistress."

With that, Chef Holst took over, as was the plan, in telling them of the ingredients and special aspects of the food and wine they were dining on. Jack Hamata returned to the table, assuring everyone that Akachan had gone immediately to sleep when he'd put her in bed, and the meal progressed in general chitchat until their deserts arrived—a choice of caramel parfait with "Lebkuchen" on champagne sabayon or a "Glühwein" poached pear with hazelnut merengue (or, for the gluttons, of which there always are many on a cruise, both).

Although Hahn had whispered to the diners separately that protocol dictated that the captain leave the table first—and he didn't linger far into the coffee and port service following the desert—Hattie Timmons had already muttered something about indigestion and risen from the table and stomped off. Irene Summersdale almost defiantly remained at the table, and when Charlotte's party left, she went into the lounge with them.

The Eberhardts left almost on the tail of the captain's departure, Hans not able to make eye contact with Charlotte, and Candace jangled off in her frosting of glittery diamonds soon after, Felix in tow. The Hamatas were there physically, but on another planet in spirit. They were whispering to each other in Japanese and then, after Mary whispered something about checking on the baby, they too drifted away.

The novelist, Bernie Colson, and his companion Sean Richards, stayed on, even after Chance suggested it was time for his foursome to retire to the Neptune lounge to enjoy the music of the "Old Town Swing Band," which had been brought on board for the evening's entertainment.

As Charlotte and crew—and Irene—were rising from the table, Bernie was asking for another glass of port and Sean was asking him if he thought that was wise. To this, Bernie remarked that a glass of port was always wise.

The music in the lounge was mellow and the group of five stayed on afterward, Charlotte enjoying a daily special Kir Royal and Brenda a Cuba Libre, while Chance continued with coffee and Marilyn and Irene went high road with sparkling water. Charlotte and Irene were discussing Quantico and Irene's interesting stories of what unusual items were included in the FBI library. Chance and Marilyn were talking about the information material they'd been given on Rothenburg, the next day's morning tour.

Charlotte looked up, startled, when Sean Richards bent down to them en route to leaving the lounge, and whispered, "Going for his medicine. Heart, you know."

So engrossed had she been in talking with Irene that she hadn't even noticed that Bernie and Sean had come into the lounge and taken up tub chairs in the shadows at the bow, in the same positions she had seen them in on that previous night when she'd seen the captain enter their cabin with them on the next deck below.

Why, she wondered, had Sean told them that about Bernie needing his heart pills?

She watched, as Sean returned and went to Bernie's side. He handed Bernie some pills and a glass of water, and Bernie took the pills. Then the two sat there, side by side, and hand in hand, watching the waves break over the bow of the boat in the moonlight as it motored its way toward Würzburg.

Irene left them, and Chance and Marilyn were talking about turning in. Charlotte knew it was time to get to bed too, but for the first time on the cruise, she felt mellow and completely relaxed.

At that moment, this mood was shattered by a high-pitched, prolonged scream coming from the reception foyer, and Candace Harrington rushed into the lounge, with Felix one step behind her, trying to reach her and envelop her in his arms.

"Gone. They're gone!"

"What are gone?" Chance asked in a calm voice, as Marilyn moved to Candace and took her hands in hers. Rico was briefly seen at the entrance to the lounge and then turned heel and was gone. Bernie and Sean turned in their seats at the bow, but they merely sat there, as onlookers. The only other person in the lounge at this late hour was the bartender, who stood there dumbly watching the scene unfold.

"My diamonds. They're gone."

"They're not gone," Chance said. "You're still wearing them."

And indeed, she was still as dripping in diamonds now as she had been at dinner.

"No, dammit," Candace cried out. "These are paste. The real ones. They were in the safe in our room. They're gone."

At that point, Captain Jorgenson strode into the room, having been fetched by Rico, who was moving in his wake.

Chance, Marilyn, and Felix concentrated on calming Candace down, as the captain turned to Charlotte and said, "I believe it is time that we need to talk, Miss Diamond. I think I need your help."

Chapter Six: Day Four: Würzburg

"So, O.W. stands for Oscar Wilde?"

Chance looked startled for a moment and then laughed. "You caught me. I didn't think any of you would see it."

"See what?" Marilyn asked.

"That the novelist, Bernard Colson is gay?" Brenda said.

"Yeah," Chance said, giving Brenda a funny look.

"Well, in my business. . . ." Brenda didn't have to complete the sentence.

"I knew it in the back of my mind," said Charlotte, who had broached the topic while sipping on the Christmas Eve special—a Bloody Mary for some obtuse reason—as they sat in the Neptune lounge after the nearly all-day tour to Rothenburg had returned. "It was pretty much confirmed when I was on the Internet while you folks were gone on the tour. He writes gay novels—pretty steamy too, I gather. And that ends one of the mysteries I was seeing."

"Oh, you are seeing mysteries on this cruise?" Marilyn asked.

"Of course she is, Marilyn, can't you see the glow about her?" Brenda asked. "She's suddenly alive and energized. She has mysteries to solve. Speaking of which, have you found your watch yet, Chance?"

"No, no, I haven't."

"There you go." Brenda again. "There's one mystery right there. But that's not the mystery you're referring to, is it Charlotte?"

"No, I'm afraid not. I had seen Captain Jorgenson with Colson and Richards several times—in odd places—and it was somewhat of a mystery why the captain put Colson beside him at the captain's welcome dinner rather than Candace or Sophia. But now I figure I know why."

"Because Captain Jorgenson is gay too—and probably reads Colson's novels?" Brenda asked.

"Yes."

"Oh, my," Marilyn contributed breathlessly.

"And apparently Chance saw it first," Charlotte continued, with a chuckle. "Thus the nicknames."

"Oh, my," Marilyn repeated.

To change the subject, Charlotte asked the other three how the tour of Rothenburg had gone.

"You really missed something," Brenda said. "It was a beautiful little moated and walled town right out of the Middle Ages, complete with spectacular views of it as we were driving down from a hill and crossing a small river."

"And the shopping was great," Marilyn added. "They were breaking down their Christmas market, so they were almost giving the handicrafts away. You should have seen how Candace Harrington had her Felix weighed down—and the Hamatas were loading up as well."

"The architecture was superb," chimed in Chance, "and the *Bier* wasn't bad either."

"And speaking of purchases," Marilyn picked up the conversation, "I'd best see if there's any room left in our cabin to stash mine—and go looking for Dietrich. He said there'd be a chance to mail purchases home and help with getting them wrapped. He said the postal people would come right on board to help us with getting them properly prepared and postmarked. Coming, Chance?"

"Yes, dear. But only as far as the bed in the cabin. There's nothing else on until the Christmas Eve gala dinner and the church services for those of us who want to be bussed back into Würzburg at eleven. It's a real shame that you didn't go into Rothenburg with us, Droopydrawers."

Charlotte growled at his use of the hated nickname as Chance and his wife gathered up Marilyn's purchases and headed for their cabin. They and Brenda had seen Charlotte in the lounge—having barely returned to the vessel herself—when they boarded on their return from the tour, and none of them had been back to their cabins yet.

"You didn't really miss not being on the tour, did you?" Brenda asked, when Charlotte's brother and sister-in-law had departed.

"No, I didn't. I managed to fill in the time, and I'm just waiting now for all hell to break out here."

"What do you mean?"

"Everyone's cabin—in fact the whole boat—was searched while you were gone."

"Searched?"

"Yes, it's the real reason I stayed behind. I didn't really have a headache this morning. There was work to do. All the proper warrants were obtained for the searches, so no one has legal recourse."

"Yes, I could tell you were faking the headache . . . now don't give me that look. I'm an actress, you know—and you clearly aren't. I just decided if you wanted to stay behind, you had that right. Besides, I knew you were sleuthing."

"You knew?"

"Yes, of course," Brenda said, with a sigh. "I had already said it. There was a glow and a rising of your energy levels about you. You really do love investigating, don't you? There are mysteries within mysteries on this boat, and you're in seventh heaven, aren't you?"

"Yes, I guess I am."

"And so you can appreciate why, although I declare I'm giving all of the movie work up, that occasionally I want to dip back into it?"

"Yes, of course. And I thought we'd already agreed that you would go down to Florida in the early spring for that White Orchid movie you want to help with."

"And you'll go with me and help flesh out a mystery plot for it? You'll be doing something you love; I know you will."

"Yes, yes, of course."

"We are much alike, Charlotte. Neither of us will really retire. We both love what we chose to do in life. And I don't want you to stop. I knew Marilyn, at least, would have wheedled you to go on the

85

tour today for any excuse short of sickness. So, it was fine with me that you said you were ill. I knew you'd be doing something you loved instead. I was just jealous that I couldn't have stayed with you. And I hope you can tell me what you did and what you found out. Like what is this about the boat being searched, and, while we're at it, who are those three goons who keep showing up in the dining room and sitting in the corners and staring everyone down? They give me the creeps. Surely, keen observer that you are, you've noticed them."

"Yes," Charlotte laughed. "They were near the top of my agenda this morning. The captain and I met and set some things in motion. There have been entirely too many thefts on the boat."

"Right. The thefts. Do you think those three goons are involved?"

"It was a possibility, but, no, they've come out clean on anything like that. They had a good reason for being here. Captain Jorgenson gave me the passenger manifest and sent me ashore to the Länder police department in Würzburg, where, even though it's Christmas Eve, I was set up with communications back to the States and on the Internet. While I rousted out help from my old FBI office and did some research of my own on the Internet, a senior Länder police detective arranged for a full search warrant on the *Rhine Maiden*. He came back here with an army of policeman who have gone through everything, including all of the passenger's cabins. Nearly everyone was on the tour, so the search was efficient and thorough—and a complete surprise."

"So, what did they find?"

"Practically nothing. At least nothing criminal. I did hear a bit about sex toys in the Harrington cabin, but . . . all very mysterious that none of the missing jewelry was found. But I digress. You asked about the three goons. They all are bodyguards. Well, the two younger men are also chauffeurs—those two are with the Eberhardts, and they are the ones who have been arranging for limousines for Hans and Sophia to take them off to wherever they've gone rather than on the land tours. My office is still checking into Hans, but those young men were booked with his party. The same with the older thug, Sam Green. He works for Candace Harrington. It appears she's had a bodyguard for years. He was booked the same time she and Felix Satoris were."

"That doesn't actually mean that any of the three is cleared of suspicion on the robberies, does it?"

"No, certainly not. But I was afraid that there was something more sinister going on here and that they were involved—that we might have a kidnapping or a dead body or two. I'd say they all have their hands full watching their clients and wouldn't see it as in their interests to be thieving on the side."

Brenda laughed. "Still not prepared to give up on your Chance Diamond curse scenario, are you?"

"No," Charlotte answered, with a laugh.

"You'll just have to settle for mere jewelry robbery then, I guess."

"Yes, maybe. That and drugs too. Although it's early days yet."

"Drugs."

"Yes, Chance noted the other day that drugs were missing from the infirmary too—a lot of them. The captain was going to get them replaced today, and . . . ah, there he is now."

Captain Jorgenson walked directly from the entrance of the lounge over to Charlotte.

"Good, there you are, Miss Diamond. I have been looking for you. The police inspector, Franz Frieden, told me he had talked with you when you returned to the boat and let you know nothing was found. I was settling him in a cabin downstairs. Luckily, we have a few empty passenger compartments. He and several uniformed policemen are going to be traveling with us now to help us solve this theft mystery. It will be difficult now to keep this from the notice of the passengers."

"Yes, I can see that," Charlotte answered. The three of them were increasingly being made aware of the heightening of the tension in the lounge as passengers moved into the room from their cabins, not only to gather before the gala dinner, but also because they had slowly become informed that the boat had been searched—that even their own cabins had been thoroughly inspected.

And the passengers uniformly weren't pleased. The captain was getting some dirty looks, and passengers were milling about near where he was sitting with Charlotte and Brenda, seemingly waiting for a turn to speak their minds to him. Irene Summersdale, on the other side of the lounge, was fighting a losing battle to calm Hattie Timmons down. It was only a matter of moments before Hattie saw the captain, and seeing him already in conversation with Charlotte and Brenda wasn't going to be enough to keep her from marching down on him.

"It looks like you are going to be busy in a few minutes, Captain," Charlotte murmured. "Did you manage to get the drugs supply restocked? I ask because Chance said something about needing more drugs for Mrs. Melard soon. She's stable, he said, but in rather a delicate condition. She hasn't been out of her cabin since that incident at breakfast the other morning."

"Yes, I've sent one of the crew into town to pick them up. Our offices contacted a doctor here who managed to do the prescribing and get a pharmacy open to fill the prescriptions."

"A crew member? Which one, may I ask?"

"Rico Ruiz. He's one of the dining room staff. I'm sure he has served you."

"Shit."

"Excuse me?"

"Sorry. I get profane when the roof collapses. Has Rico returned to the ship yet?"

"Not to my knowledge. Why?"

"In my checking this afternoon, I found that Rico Ruiz has a record. He is a convicted thief. And he has convictions for drug possession and use."

"*Scheiss*." This time it was the captain speaking.

"And he's not the only one. The man with Candace Harrington, Felix Satoris. He's been convicted of theft too. For jewel theft. We need to check whether there is any connection between those two—and we need to send the police out to try to find Rico."

Any further discussion was cut off by Hattie Timmons, cutting her way through the other passengers gathering around the captain. "Captain Jorgenson. I have a bone to pick with you."

* * * *

"The old battle-ax is probably beyond embarrassment at having a policeman finding that she has holes in her bloomers."

"Chance Diamond. Behave yourself." The admonishment came from Marilyn.

The four of them were sitting in the Lorelei dining room, in the middle of a riot of streamers, balloons, noise makers, and free-flowing wine. It was the gala Christmas Eve dinner aboard the *Rhine Maiden*, especially festive to hide the fact that the boat would be moored here through tomorrow too without any special activities on land because it was Christmas and Germany was celebrating that in private family gatherings, shops shuttered tight, regardless of the high-paying guests in their midst.

The noise was almost beyond the capability of conversation, even with tablemates, and everyone was in a convivial mood, the unpleasantness of the violation of their private lives while they were on tour forgotten, or at least placed in suspension as long as the food and wine was plentiful. Well, nearly everyone. Malcolm Melard had put in an appearance and was sitting with Irene Summersdale and Hattie Timmons—as was the tour director, Dietrich Hahn, no doubt sitting there to placate Hattie Timmons. This was, of course, a losing battle. She was as sour as ever, and both Irene and Malcolm looked uncomfortable and embarrassed that their table was being a dour island of discontent in the middle of a sea of frivolity.

Even Candace Harrington, who had every reason to be devastated by the loss of a fortune in jewels, was partying like there was no tomorrow—all aglitter in her costume jewelry. She, backed up by a garishly costumed Pierre Pelletier and Felix Satoris taking up the caboose, was weaving around between the tables to the sound of the music and trying to start up a conga line.

The Hamatas were there, looking a little confused about what Christmas Eve was all about. But they, of course, had little Akachan, seated between them at a table, to focus on. They had picked a table at the center of the room, and Mary was "feeding" the Cabbage Patch doll. Taken up in the spirit of the day and the festivities, diners were stopping by their table and cooing at the little one and treating it like it was a real child—which had both Jack and Mary beaming and Jack glad handing and embracing everyone who stopped by to play their little game with them.

"I do believe Akachan is putting on weight," Brenda leaned into Charlotte and said. This was accompanied by her special form of tinkling laughter.

"What? I can't hear you," Charlotte bellowed back.

Brenda leaned farther in and spoke louder. "I said I think that even Akachan is putting on weight on the cruise. She looks fatter every day—just like the rest of us. They feed us too well."

"Yeah, right," Charlotte shot back. She was preparing to say something else, though, when a cry of distress rang out over the hubbub of the festive celebration.

91

All eyes turned on a middle-aged woman in a green satin dress near the center of the room.

"It's gone. My mother's bracelet is gone. I know I had it on when I came to dinner."

Nearly all eyes turned on her, focused on her obvious distress.

The eyes of Captain Jorgenson and Charlotte, however, met each others'. Their distress was no less than that of the woman in the green dress. Rico had been off the boat since early in the afternoon and still had not returned or been found. So much assumption had been pinned on the likelihood that he was the jewel thief.

Shifting her gaze from Jorgenson, Charlotte immediately began scanning the room to place key people—not the least, where the caboose of the conga line was—Felix Satoris.

Chapter Seven: Days Five through Eight: Würzburg to Koblenz

"It's pleasant here, gently rocking and watching the lights of the city gradually go out. I'm glad they dimmed the lights in the lounge. The tree they brought in and trimmed this afternoon makes all the difference in the mood."

Brenda was looking over at the trimmed and lit Christmas tree at the edge of the dance floor in the Neptune lounge. The overhead lights had been dimmed so that the lights on the tree stood out even more than they had earlier, at the break of Christmas morning, when an impromptu Christmas Eve service had been held here.

"That was good of you to volunteer to conduct a service, Marilyn," Charlotte said, reaching over and patting her sister-in-law on the knee. "I know that many were disappointed that Detective Frieden quarantined the boat after the incident in the dining room, preventing us from taking the scheduled trips to churches in the city. And I know that your offer to go ahead and conduct a service in here was appreciated and calmed them. The calm before the storm."

"The storm?" Chance asked. "You've seen a weather forecast for tomorrow—umm, I mean today?"

"I think she means the storm that's brewing on this boat—the jewelry thefts," clarified Brenda.

"I had no idea how many people were missing items," Marilyn said. "Mary Hamata seemed quite distressed when she reported that she was missing hair combs embedded with sapphires."

"Which only brings up once again the question of why people take valuable jewelry on trips like this," Charlotte said, with a slight snort of derision.

"I know jewelry doesn't mean that much to you, Charlotte, and of course there's no reason why it should. But it has meaning for many people, and the world has become so informal—there are very few places to wear valuable jewelry anymore. And a cruise like this is a time to put on the dog. There are the captain's gala dinners. Did you see how many men were wearing tuxedos the other night? Those are a nuisance to bring on a cruise for just one or two meals—but it's all part of the ambiance."

"And not all of the items taken were simply expensive baubles," Marilyn chimed in. "Other people are missing wristwatches, just like Chance is."

"I have other watches," Chance said "—and insurance will cover that one. I'll bet Candace Harrington won't be crying too much over her lost diamonds, either. I'm sure those are insured up to the hilt. And she had the sensible, albeit expensive, answer to the risk problem. Those paste replicas she had made look like the real thing."

"Which begs the question of why she didn't just bring the paste ones and leave the real ones in a bank vault," Charlotte said.

"Oh, Char," Marilyn murmured.

Charlotte was going to say something further, but movement in her peripheral vision caught her eye and she looked up. The young man, Sean Richards, was brushing by them, headed toward the entrance to the lounge. As on previous nights, Richards and his older friend, Bernie Colson, had been sitting close together in tub chairs at the window of the lounge overlooking the bow of the boat. A few other couples and singles were scattered about the lounge too, observing the movement of time into Christmas morning. All were subdued and mellow, though—mellow, in all probability, because of the feast and drink they'd had at the Christmas Eve gala and in contemplation of their Christmases of past years and subdued by the police lockdown of the boat. Tomorrow they would face another round of searches and questions. The boat hadn't been scheduled to leave Würzburg until the next night anyway, but because it was Christmas Day, no other activities had been planned for the passengers either. All were concerned about how long the boat would be detained here, and what that meant for the rest of the cruise they had been looking forward to.

As he passed—and as he had on a previous occasion—Richards leaned down to Charlotte and said, "Have to get Bernie's heart medicine again. I swear he's going to forget it and pop off one of these days."

Charlotte just smiled wanly and nodded her head. But she wondered if the young man broadcast to everyone on the *Rhine Maiden* that Bernard Colson had heart problems.

Chance rose from his seat and went up to the bow and sat down next to Colson while Richards was gone. The doctor and the novelist spoke in quiet tones.

None of the others of Charlotte's party spoke until after Chance returned when he saw that Richards was drifting back into the room with pills and a glass of water.

As Chance rejoined his foursome, he looked a bit perplexed, but he didn't say anything other than that he was tired and ready to turn in. Marilyn was ready to leave, as well. When the two of them had gone, Brenda moved her chair closer to Charlotte's, and the two of them snuggled up.

"So calm and peaceful," Brenda murmured.

"The calm before the storm."

"You've said that already. Do you really think that something is going to break?"

"At least in some of the mysteries, yes," Charlotte said. "But this is all so complex, and I keep thinking there are answers running right across the screen before my eyes—and that I'm just not seeing the picture in full focus."

"It must be frustrating."

"Yes and no. Yes, because I am anxious to see the end of it and no because when I feel like this, I'm usually close to bringing it all into focus."

"Inconvenient, wasn't it?" Brenda asked with a sigh after a few moments of silence.

"What was inconvenient?"

"Inconvenient that whoever took that woman's bracelet at dinner . . . you are sure that's when she lost it, aren't you?"

"Yes. Her husband said he helped with the clasp before dinner, and a woman at her table declared that she had admired the bracelet and spoken to the woman about it during dinner."

"Well then, inconvenient, I think for whoever is stealing the jewelry that they didn't know that the waiter who has absconded was already under suspicion for that. They could have just stopped at the point and the suspicion would all be on Rico, wouldn't it?"

"Yes, that's a good way of putting it."

"Unless, of course, there is a connection between Candace Harrington's younger man, Felix, and Rico."

"None has been found yet by the FBI. Although you can bet that Felix will face quite an interrogation in the morning. They not only have different tastes in robbery, but they also have been operating on difference continents, with no apparent linking. I like that, however—how you put it. An inconvenient robbery. I think that might help me bring this into focus. But I'm tired now. What do you say that we fade off to bed?"

"I thought you'd never ask."

* * * *

Christmas morning was a sluggish one aboard the *Rhine Maiden*. Many of the passengers probably wouldn't have gotten up at all until the afternoon if Franz Frieden of the Bavarian Länder Polizei and his men weren't rousting them out for repeat inspections of their cabins for the stolen jewelry—the list of which was rather extensive now—and for some detailed questioning. The procedure had started on the lowest deck, and started with the crew cabins, so the first-class passengers weren't approached until nearly noon. None except for Candace Harrington and her boy toy were actually still in their cabins that late, though. Most couldn't sleep past the time the inspectors reached the cabin of Irene Summersdale and Hattie Timmons and Hattie began to let the whole world know how much she was enjoying this experience.

Perhaps the most disgruntled passenger over this indignity, however, was Hans Eberhardt, who, with his wife, Sophia, retired to the captain's bridge—much to the chagrin of Captain Jorgenson, and placed his now-acknowledged young chauffer bodyguards between him and the door.

Both Chance and Charlotte had been up at the crack of dawn, although their mates were sleeping in a bit longer. Chance had wanted to check with the Melards, and after he did, he went to the captain, who made calls and was able, even though it was Christmas morning, to find a doctor in the town who would provide the drugs Chance needed to continue the treatment of Doris Melard. Over coffee, Charlotte pressed him on how she was doing and all Chance would say was that it was somewhat of a mystery, that she should be doing better than she seemed to be doing. He said that he had recommended to both Malcolm Melard and Captain Jorgenson that she be taken from the ship and put in a hospital, preferable a major one, which Jorgenson said they wouldn't reach until they got to Koblenz in four days. Chance thought she would be able to hold until then—that, indeed, he didn't know why she was so lethargic now.

Charlotte was up early because Frank Frieden had welcomed her assistance and gave her free access to his investigation. The other passengers didn't know this, though—except, of course, for Charlotte's own party—so she was able to mingle and catch conversations and somewhat bald responses to what was happening.

While his men searched the *Rhine Maiden* from top to bottom yet again, Frieden set up shop in the crew's dining room, where, one by one, he interviewed all of the passengers and crew members. Charlotte was checking in at this room when she encountered and was passed by two people, a man and a woman, in business suits and looking very official. She hadn't seen either one of them on the boat before.

"Those two here just now?" Frieden asked. "Those are insurance investigators. Christmas or not, the worth of Mrs. Harrington's lost jewelry has brought them out. They had to drive over from Frankfurt, or they would have been here yesterday."

"Did they give you any idea what the jewels are worth?"

"They said they were insured for something in the neighborhood of one and a half-million U.S. dollars."

"Quite a heist. A bit higher league than some of the watches and bits and pieces of jewelry on the stolen list."

"Yes, a real windfall for our thief," Frieden said.

"Hmmm," was Charlotte's response. And she was about to say something, when a policeman appeared at the door and started jabbering excitedly to Frieden in German.

Frieden answered in German and then turned to Charlotte and said, "They have apprehended this waiter, this Rico Ruiz. He was halfway to Frankfurt already. I will go now and meet the authorities in the town in which he was apprehended, and we will see what we see with this young man."

Charlotte walked back up to the top level of the vessel with Frieden and saw him off down the gang plank. As she was returning to her cabin, she could see the insurance investigators sitting with Candace Harrington in the Neptune lounge. Flanking her were Felix and Sophia Eberhardt. For some reason that tableau struck Charlotte as unusual. She didn't know why it would. She'd seen Candace and Felix leaving with the Eberhardts in a limousine while the *Rhine Maiden* was still docked in Nürnberg before this unexpected journey of perplexity had begun. But then at least part of the picture began to come into focus. Other than that outing and the captain's dinner—the attendance at which was established by the ship's staff—Charlotte hadn't seen Candace with the Eberhardts. They hadn't been traveling companions in any sense of the word as Charlotte and Brenda and the Diamonds had been. And yet here was Sophia, holding Candace's hand while Candace was speaking with the insurance adjustors about her missing jewelry to the tune of a million and a half dollars.

Franz Frieden returned to the boat during the dinner hour. He caught Charlotte's eye while she was eating, but she just nodded slightly and he withdrew. The passengers had been antsy all afternoon.

100

If the search had turned up anything, no one had been told that it had, and buzz went around the boat when Frieden abruptly left—unfortunately just as Hattie Timmons had been summoned for her interview with him. She, of course, said that he had retreated before her, unable to justify all of this indignity they had been forced to suffer.

The rumor that seemed to be upsetting them the most was the suggestion that the cruise effectively was over—that they'd be held here for days and eventually just sent straight home after the culprit had been caught. Someone in the crew had now revealed that one of the crew members—the waiter Rico Ruiz—had absconded, and the betting was that he was the thief and that the cruise would quickly be canceled—and that their valuables would never be recovered. Crew members had fanned the rumor of the cruise cancellation by cheerfully noting that if the boat's schedule at the locks along the waterways went off by even a couple of hours, the *Rhine Maiden*'s progress schedule would be disrupted too long for the cruise to proceed.

"Excuse me, I'm off to the ladies' room," Charlotte murmured to her tablemates after waiting a decent amount of time since she had spied Frieden in the doorway.

"Give our regards to Detective Frieden," Chance said.

"Shhh, keep it down. We don't want it generally known that I'm working with him."

"Of course, dear sister, if you tell us all you find out when you return."

"What, and breach professional privilege?" Charlotte countered. Then, as three faces gave her silly expressions, she got up and left. She was still seething a bit that Chance invoked doctor-patient privilege with Doris Melard. Charlotte very much wanted to know what was really wrong with Doris, how wrong it was, and what her husband might be doing to either help or hinder her. In the back of her mind she couldn't help but believe there was something she should be doing about this—or should know about.

"Did he confess to the thefts?" Charlotte asked as soon as she entered Frieden's temporary office.

"Only to the drug thefts," Frieden said. "He declared that he had no idea about any jewelry thefts, and we found no evidence of that on him. Of course he'd had more than a day to stash it all away. I left one of my detectives to continue grilling him. I had to get back here."

"You discovered something that made you need to be back here?" Charlotte asked.

"It's not that. I've been given permission to follow and develop this case even beyond the Länder boundaries. The *Rhine Maiden* can sail on its established schedule. The authorities don't want to disrupt tourism any more than absolutely necessary. The land tours can start up again too. Life here can go on as normal, except that my men will be watching—and so, I hope, will you—without the passengers knowing you are."

"That's good news—about the cruise continuing," Charlotte said. "That will calm down the passengers a good bit now. And I'll bet the robberies end. The presence of the policemen will see to that. But tell me, do you really think that Rico Ruiz is enough of a thief to be stealing diamonds and emeralds? That normally takes access to a very good fence operation. I read his file, and I'm not sure he's our man. The drugs, yes. But he's already confessed to that."

"No, we know the robbing didn't end with the departure of our young waiter. I think we still have a thief among us—a much higher-level and much more dangerous and clever thief than Rico Ruiz is."

* * * *

The passengers perked up when they felt the *Rhine Maiden* rev up its engines that night near midnight and begin to nudge its way out into the water. Until then, many had hung around the lounge, hanging their heads and feeding the various rumors in hushed tones in small discussion groups.

Charlotte didn't tell her own group that they would proceed with the cruise as scheduled until after Marilyn had noticed the rumbling of the engines. She didn't want them to show to the other passengers a lack of concern about what was happening.

By morning, when they woke up and found the *Rhine Maiden* docked in the town of Wertheim, life for the vacationers had almost returned to normal. Sure, the policemen were still there, but they were being unobtrusive enough—not getting in anyone's way—the interviews had ceased, and nearly everyone was happy to be convinced that the missing waiter was the thief. The rumor had even been circulated that he'd been caught and had confessed and that all of the missing jewelry would be returned at the end of the voyage in Amsterdam.

The morning started off with a glassblowing demonstration, which Charlotte fully and, at least on the surface, gaily, participated in. She didn't want anyone to associate her with the somber policemen standing around—and she wanted to gather whatever tidbits of information she could in mingling. She even made a glass vase that she thought would look very good in the den back at Brenda's house in Hopewell—and another one that she could give to Sherry as part of the thank-you for watching the dogs for them. That Brenda laughed at them and had to be told they were vases didn't matter to Charlotte one jot; Brenda's attempts had just imploded upon themselves. Charlotte was delighted that there was something in the realm of the arts she could do better than Brenda could—if only marginally better.

That afternoon they were all welcomed on a walking tour of the sixteenth-century town of Wertheim, with its period-typical half-timbered houses located on narrow, winding streets in the shadow of a mighty fortress on the hill. Here they went to a famous glass museum, where they could compare their own efforts of the morning with museum-quality pieces—and, of course, have the opportunity to buy the latter. The last stop was a winery, where they all received a lecture and tasting on the wines of the Baden-Württemberg region and where Chance received the amused laughter of most and baleful looks from Jack Hamata when he pointed out that the Cabbage Patch doll, Akachan, perpetually in the Hamata's company, was too young to drink the wine and thus Jack would have to take the "baby" out of the wine-tasting room. Jack initially went red in the face, but then he picked up on the game and did, indeed, exit the winery with Akachan. Hattie Timmons added to the stifled amusement of the others in the group by tapping, none too lightly, Jack on the shins as he and Akachan departed and then thumping down on the bench beside Mary Hamata in the space that Jack had earlier refused to remove the doll from so Hattie could sit.

If anyone in the waves of groups from the boat who took the walking tour noticed that they seemed to all be kept together and within sight by the policemen who accompanied the groups, no one noticed—or at least no one remarked on it.

What Charlotte did notice, however, was that neither Candace Harrington and her Felix nor the Eberhardts took the walking tour. And the two couples, following Sophia's brief attentions to Candace the previous day in the lounge, seemed to have split off again, as if they didn't even know each other. They had appeared at the entrance of the Lorelei restaurant both the previous night for dinner and then again this morning for breakfast and, without acknowledging the presence of each other, had gone off to sit at separate tables.

Chance had convinced Malcolm Melard that he needed the exercise of taking the tour and the waitress, Gretchen, had happily agreed to sit with Deloris Melard while he accompanied the others to Wertheim. Bernie Colson and Sean Richards were there, but they lagged a bit behind the rest because of Bernie's need to use his cane. But Charlotte noticed that he seemed to be brushing off Richards's continuous attempts to help him along—as if he didn't think he was as debilitated as Richards thought he was.

It was later that afternoon, as the passengers were returning to the *Rhine Maiden*, that the storm that Charlotte had anticipated and longed for started to break.

As she boarded the ship, a policeman pulled her aside and whispered that Franz Frieden wanted to see her urgently in the crew dining room.

Charlotte didn't know what to expect while she was descending two levels to the crew quarters, but she couldn't say she was surprised when she found out what Frieden had to tell her. Somewhere in the back of her mind, this was already coming together.

"Has Rico Ruiz confessed to the jewelry thefts?" she asked as she entered the small room.

"No, and I don't think he will. He insists he only went after the drugs, and we just can't connect him with jewelry thefts. These are two entirely different MOs."

"I agree. So why do you look so agitated."

"It's the banker and his Italian wife and that American rich heiress and her boyfriend. And the three bodyguards as well. My men didn't even notice until the limousine was already pulling away. They even had members of the boat's crew trundling their luggage off the vessel and helping to see that my men were looking the other way. It happened quickly, and they must have paid the crew members well, because we're giving them the workover they probably knew we would—and that they certainly deserve."

"The Eberhardts and Candace Harrington are gone?"

"Yes, it would appear so. I had instructed everyone in no uncertain terms that the cruise would go on—if a bit more supervised than usual—but that they were all to stay with the cruise. And now seven of them are gone."

"You need to ask the insurance investigators if Harrington has receipts on file for the paste versions of her stolen diamonds."

"I don't follow." And Frieden certainly did look perplexed. "What does that have to do with—?"

"I should have suspected it earlier, what with the four being chummy at the beginning and then again later and acting like they didn't even know each other otherwise. And Candace flaunting those diamonds like she did. That was a nice, gutsy touch. And I bet she's roped in Felix Satoris more for his jewelry thief background than because he pleases her so well in bed."

"Excuse me? My English isn't so good, but . . ."

"Put out an order to track that limousine down and hold them all. That's what I strongly suggest," Charlotte said. "I think you'll find that the diamonds Candace has with her aren't paste—they are the real ones. I think the paste ones don't exist and that, with the help of her own gigolo and a shyster Swiss banker, Candace Harrington is trying to have her diamonds and be paid the insurance on them as well. I think those are our diamond thieves."

When he had recovered and put out an order to track down the fleeing banker and heiress, Frieden addressed Charlotte again. "And you think they took the other jewelry as well? Maybe Felix being a little sticky fingered on the side?"

"Perhaps," Charlotte answered. "But again, perhaps not. My friend, Brenda, said something the other night that I realized was important—but maybe it was more important than I thought. She indicated that maybe Ruiz's theft of the drugs was an inconvenient robbery, as it placed focus on the more important robbery—the

107

million and a half dollars in diamonds. But maybe, just maybe, there have been more inconvenient robberies than that. We'll have to see—and I want to get to the Internet to do some research again. Perhaps as far as Harrington goes, you could have your people start checking into whether her finances are liquid or if she needed some fairly quick cash."

* * * *

That night the *Rhine Maiden* was on the move again, this time to Frankfurt, where Charlotte didn't get a chance to do much Internet browsing, between messaging back and forth with her former assistant at the FBI Annapolis office, Margaret Fancel, and being included in an interrogation of Rico Ruiz, who had been brought to Frankfurt for Franz Frieden to reinterview. After hearing Ruiz being questioned again, both Frieden and Charlotte were convinced that his thieving was limited to the drugs.

The police had found the limousine the Eberhardts and Candace Harrington had escaped in the previous day. But only four people—the three bodyguards and Felix Satoris—had been found with the car. Charlotte was sure—and Frieden reluctantly agreed—that the Eberhardts were already safely back in Switzerland and were untouchable. They also agreed that Harrington could be almost anywhere and was equally untouchable. That didn't really matter that much. The insurance company hadn't cut a check for the loss of the diamonds—and now wouldn't, because they agreed with Charlotte that they'd have to see an awfully convincing post-dated receipt for paste versions before they would now acknowledge that there had been a theft at all. Harrington being Harrington, the insurance company wouldn't pursue a charge of swindling; they'd quietly cancel their policies with her—and just be amused if another company got taken by her.

Poor Felix was just out of luck. He sang like a bird, having been abandoned by Harrington, and acknowledged that he'd told her how she could pull it off and that Hans Eberhardt had been along for the instruction on how it was done. But, there being no actual crime anyone was pursuing, Felix was just tumbled out onto the streets of Frankfurt, penniless, at the end of the morning—with the Frankfurt Polizei being informed that a needy jewel theft was in their city. The one thing Felix had been steadfast in insisting, though, was that he had had nothing to do with stealing anything—that even Harrington's diamonds hadn't been stolen.

Upon hearing this, Charlotte had muttered, "An inconvenient robbery," to which Satoris had said, "What?" But she saw no reason to explain that. She believed him when he said he hadn't stolen the jewelry.

The three thug bodyguards were probably more fortunate. Their employers would pay well to have them back at their sides again.

The one piece of useful information that Charlotte got back from her e-mail exchanges with Margaret Fancel was confirmation that Harrington wasn't financially liquid and did seem to need cash. If she'd had more time and actually had had paste versions made—and maybe safely hidden away in one of Hans Eberhardt's bank vaults, maybe she would have gotten away with her swindle.

Before Charlotte could get to work on the Internet, though, she and Frieden had to be back in a car headed for Mainz—because that's where the *Rhine Maiden* was repositioned over the morning from Frankfurt.

The rest of the passengers who were able and interested in touring had been put on busses in Frankfurt and driven to Heidelberg that morning for a tour of the famous mountain-top castle there. When Chance, Marilyn, and Brenda got back to the ship in Mainz from that tour, they were all aglow with what a great castle that was—and anxious to tell Charlotte about the "incident of Hattie and the staircase," as the event would come to be known. Almost unable to transmit the story to Charlotte coherently through their laughter, they told her of how Hattie, who, of course, opted for the regular rather than the easy tour, got stuck in a narrow tower staircase in the upper reaches of Heidelberg Castle and had to be yanked out of there from the top, butt first—and then proceeded to refuse to try to go down the stairs again, insisting that she be taken to the elevator which, of course, she's been quite specifically told didn't exist. Before the tour, the escorts had quite clearly told them there was no way up or down other than that narrow spiral staircase.

Through her laughter, Charlotte asked, "I wonder if Bernie Colson tried that."

"Oh, he didn't go on the tour," Marilyn answered. "Sean Richards took it, but he told me that Bernie had had heart palpitations this morning and decided not to go."

"Funny," Chance said. "I talked to Colson before the tours left this morning, and he told me he was staying behind because he wanted to work on a novel manuscript—that he'd been to Heidelberg several times already."

"Hmmm," Charlotte said.

That night, in the lounge, all were happy and gay. Each day that went by without the passengers seeing anything bad happen to them was one more day of seeing life return to normal and of getting the full tour they had all paid so dearly for. Chance and Marilyn were completely taken up in this mood and didn't seem to notice that Charlotte, sipping on her special of the day, a Green Widow, was being very contemplative—while Brenda, trying to deal with the other special, which she regretted ordering, a Madras, was both trying to match the mood of the Diamonds and the other passengers and to keep a watchful eye on Charlotte.

∗ ∗ ∗ ∗

The afternoon of day eight of the cruise saw the *Rhine Maiden* docked at the small wine-producing eleventh-century town of Rüdesheim, where the touring passengers visited the Brömserberg Castle and two wineries. It was also where they'd been told they would be helped to mail their Christmas Market packages home. Marilyn had spent the late morning, while the *Rhine Maiden* was steaming from Mainz to Rüdesheim, in the lounge where all those who wanted them were provided packing boxes, wrapping materials, and help in addressing their packages.

As soon as they hit Rüdesheim, however, Charlotte, in the company of one of Franz Frieden's detectives, was off to the local police station to use their Internet. She was both perplexed and flushed with interesting, if not wholly understandable, information and some sense of how to help Frieden wrap up this robbery investigation.

"You missed some good wineries again," Chance told Charlotte when she returned to the *Rhine Maiden* late in the afternoon.

"Did you have to throw the Hamatas' baby, Akachan, out of the wine room again?" Charlotte asked.

"No, they didn't have Akachan today," Brenda answered for Chance.

"Have we ever seen them without Akachan before?" Charlotte shot back.

"No, I don't think we ever have," Marilyn answered. "The doll was even there in the lounge this morning when the Hamatas were wrapping up their Christmas Market purchases."

"And the packages have gone off to be mailed?"

"Yes, as far as I know. We did all of the paperwork right there in the lounge and there were even postal people there, and they said they'd take it all off and put it through the mails while we were touring Rüdesheim. You seem keyed up, Charlotte. Is there anything—?"

"And do you remember seeing the doll after all of the packages were wrapped, Marilyn?" Charlotte was on a mission, focused. Everything was coming into focus for her now.

"Ummm, no, but the doll has been around so much that I didn't even notice."

"Precisely," Charlotte said in an "ah ha" voice, and then she was racing off in search of Franz Frieden.

Ten minutes later Charlotte and Frieden, backed up by several policemen, were knocking at the Hamatas' cabin door.

Jack Hamata answered the door.

"May we please see the doll you call Akachan?" Franz Frieden said when he was face to face with Jack.

"And could you tell us who you and Mary really are?" Charlotte added.

Chapter Eight: Day Nine: Koblenz

"Perhaps I should return. I expected Chance to be back by now."

"You said it was just stress-related heart palpitations, didn't you, Marilyn?" Charlotte said to her sister-in-law. "I'm surprised Irene hasn't had them before now, having to be around Hattie constantly. The rest of us have only had to take her in small doses. And you said Irene was doing much better, didn't you? I'm sure you were a help, but she probably just wants to rest now."

"Well . . ." Marilyn answered, unsure. The three women were sitting at a table in the dining room, enjoying a lunch—along with the rest of the passengers—as the *Rhine Maiden* was slowly, almost majestically, approaching Koblenz, which, like many beautiful cities was best seen from the river. They had all just enjoyed an entire morning standing or sitting at the windows of the lounge and oohing and awwing over the slow sail on the segment of the Rhine known as the "romantic Rhine," where the banks of the Rhine rose high on each side through a gorge ending at the famous rock formation called the Lorelei. Here, by legend, sirens sang to lure vessels onto the treacherous rocks below and just under the surface of the water. During the Medieval centuries, magnificent castles had been built at the tops of peaks lining this section of the Rhine—as well as toll castles perched on rocks in the middle of the river—so that an awe-inspiring structure was ever in view during their entire morning of cruising.

It was this stretch of the cruise that had been most inviting to Charlotte, and a tour guide was giving a running commentary from the bridge over the loudspeaker system on the various sites as they cruised. Thus Charlotte had turned away all enquiries from her party on what had transpired with the Hamatas the previous evening when she and Franz Frieden had interrogated them and they were taken off the ship—and their precious "child," Akachan, was retrieved from the postal system and brought back on board. From the time Charlotte returned to her cabin, she had said she couldn't say anything until lunchtime today, when Detective Frieden would be making a general announcement in the dining room.

The "romantic Rhine" section astern of them and the *Rhine Maiden* having set her bow for the entry into Koblenz, Charlotte, Brenda, Marilyn, and Chance had joined the rest of the passengers in a movement toward the Lorelei restaurant, all achatter on the magnificent sightseeing morning they had from the comfort of the vessel's lounge. They were all remarking on the need to come back and take the cruise in warmer weather, so that they could view it all from the outside deck above. As it was, some brave souls had bundled up and watched it all from there anyway.

As they had approached the dining room, a crew member stopped Chance and pulled him aside. As the two men were conversing in low tones, the three women held up as well. Chance had then come to the women and whispered that Irene Summersdale was having a heart problem—she thought—down in her cabin and that he was going to go check on her. Marilyn said she'd go too, and as Chance knew that Marilyn was a great help in calming people down, he agreed.

As they split off and headed down the stairs to the lower-deck cabin, Hattie Timmons lunged by them, sluggishly tackling the stairs with her bum leg and cane, holding up traffic headed to lunch from below and showing every evidence of not letting even the physical distress of her cabin mate keep her from the opportunity to complain about another meal on the *Rhine Maiden*.

Marilyn had come back up to the dining room, saying that Chance just thought it was stress that was causing Irene discomfort and that he'd give her a sedative and recommend that she rest. Marilyn was needed topside, he had said, more than in the cabin. She could make sure that Hattie—the probable main source of the stress—stayed away from the cabin at least long enough for Irene to get some calming rest. Thus, as the three women ate, Marilyn kept a sharp eye on Hattie's whereabouts and voiced her frustration about needing to be both up here and down on the lower deck, holding Irene's hand.

But Brenda's curiosity was bursting on another matter. "It's lunchtime, Charlotte. Tell us how you figured out that the Hamatas were stealing the jewelry and stuffing it in their doll, Akachan, to be mailed back to them in Japan."

"You provided the first clue to me, Brenda. And I then figured out another piece of the puzzle yesterday afternoon while checking on the Internet. And Marilyn provided the clincher when I returned to the boat."

"Me?" Marilyn asked in surprise, turning her face from where Hattie was, once again, telling the waitress, Gretchen, how she personally should have prepared her meal.

"Yes. It was Brenda's comment, days ago, at the Christmas Eve dinner, that I should have paid more attention to. She made a joke about how Akachan was getting fat on the food they were stuffing us with right along with everyone else. And she was right. The doll's stomach did seem to be expanding. That was because the Hamatas were stuffing the doll with all of the incidental loot they were clipping off folks they were brushing past—Chance's watch, for instance. And they just kept it in the doll and kept the doll with them, so neither of the police searches of the boat came up with anything. They didn't have Candace Harrington's diamonds at all—those were being hidden in plain sight—on Candace—posing as paste. In the same vein, the Hamatas were hiding their stolen loot in plain sight—and cleverly throwing us all off the scent by focusing us all on the doll and on their seemingly harmless idiocy in treating the doll like a human. They obviously are real pros at this."

"But if Jack is the CEO of a pharmaceutical corporation, why—?" Brenda began to ask.

"Jack Hamata is, indeed, CEO of Hamata Pharmaceuticals," Charlotte said. "But these weren't the Hamatas who were on this cruise. We don't know who they are, but they've been taken off the

Rhine Maiden in Rüdesheim and are in custody and being interrogated and fingerprinted, so we should know who they are by the end of the cruise. I found out they weren't authentic by browsing on the Internet yesterday—something I should have done earlier when the robberies started, but there never seemed to be time enough to do the research. The CEO of the pharmaceutical corporation has his bio and photo on the Net. He's in his sixties, his wife is dead, and all of his children are women in their twenties and thirties. Whoever these people are, they aren't Jack Hamata or his dead wife. Akachan certainly isn't one of the grown daughters."

"And me? What did I contribute?" Marilyn asked.

"You zeroed me in as soon as I saw you yesterday afternoon on how they were going to get away with this—and they might have gotten away with it if they weren't inconveniently stealing at the same time as Candace Harrington was swindling and Rico Ruiz was swiping drugs. Candace probably would have gotten away with what she was doing too if there hadn't inconveniently been other robberies going on. Only Rico was doomed to be picked up on the drugs issue—and even he might have managed not to be caught if police attention to the robberies hadn't flushed him out."

"But what did I do?"

"You focused me in on the Hamatas mailing purchases home and Akachan not being with them after they'd done that. With all of the attention they were focusing on that doll as being a real person, they hardly would have just wrapped her up mid cruise and shipped her away. But obviously they had to do that with all of the police scrutiny around them. If they had accounted for that, they probably

118

would have brought a second doll to replace the first one they were mailing away. But they had no idea that Candace's supposed million-and-a-half-dollar diamond heist would bring the police down on the boat. An inconvenient robbery for them. They were after cheaper, lower-profile takings."

"But why couldn't you tell us until now?" Brenda asked.

"Find out for yourself," Charlotte said, placing a hand on Brenda's arm. "I see that Franz Frieden is here now. He wanted to make the official wrap-up announcement with no chance of rumors spreading before he did so. Having the most exciting, scenic part of the cruise this morning helped to distract everyone, of course."

"Attention, please, everyone." It was Captain Jorgenson speaking, which stopped all conversation across the dining room immediately. "Detective Frieden here would like to address you all before we reach Koblenz." The boat already was moving into the center of Koblenz at this moment. And right as Frieden took the mike and started to speak, a frazzled-looking Pierre Pelletier came into the dining room and pulled on Jorgenson's sleeve, and, after Pierre whispered something in the captain's ear, they both left the dining room.

Charlotte wasn't sure whether anyone else other than her noticed this. Most of the other passengers had turned their attention to Frieden.

"As you all are aware, I'm sure," Frieden began, "The passengers on the cruise have been experiencing a spate of thefts—and I and a contingent of officers from the Bavarian Länder Polizei have been on the cruise with you for a number of days. We hope we haven't inconvenienced you appreciably, but I'm sure you also wanted the thieves caught and your personal possessions returned."

At the mention of "thieves" rather than "thief," a buzz went up in the crowd as they realized that something concrete must be known about who was doing this for the detective to use the plural. Heads started to turn and scan the room for who was missing from among the passengers and dining room crew.

"Yes, we have uncovered the thieves, you will be relieved to know," Frieden continued. "Our suspects are the Japanese couple who have been traveling with you. We don't know who they are yet, but we do know that they are not the Hamatas they were impersonating."

Pierre had returned to the restaurant, looking quite distraught, and was edging around the wall toward Charlotte's table. Catching Charlotte's eye, he motioned that she was needed.

Assuming that something had turned for the worse for Irene—especially because Chance hadn't returned yet, she quickly whispered to Brenda what she thought the problem was and that she and Marilyn needed to leave and then caught Marilyn's attention. As the two were withdrawing as unobtrusively as possible toward the entrance to the dining room where Pierre had already moved, Frieden was continuing with his announcement. As he now was addressing a subject that many in the room were closely interested in, all attention was still focused on him.

"I am happy to report that we have recovered and photographed a number of items the Japanese couple may have stolen from those among you. I have received permission to return these to you rather than holding them for trial. But I ask that those of you who are missing jewelry and other small items form a line over at that table, where those detectives are sitting. You will have to identify what is yours, have the matching photograph marked with your name, and sign a receipt. Then you may have your item back. I will . . ."

At this point, Pierre was pulling on Frieden's arm and whispering in his ear. Also, at this point, the *Rhine Maiden* started making a sharp turn to port and the motors screamed as the boat's speed picked up noticeably. They were headed straight toward the opening of the mouth of a smaller waterway, the Moselle River, and a large bronze statue of a king warrior on a sturdy steed in a park. Several of the passengers had to steady themselves at the unexpected turn and increase in speed, but none had much of a reason to think that anything was happening except a rather awkward approach to the ship's docking position.

". . . I will need to leave for a few minutes now. If you have other questions, I will leave my colleague, Gerhard Ingles, who is sitting over at the table I've already designated, in charge. Please ask him if you have any questions or if you have lost something that you can't find among the items we have."

"Is it Irene Summersdale?" Charlotte asked Pierre in a low voice when she joined him at the entrance to the dining room.

"No, it's Mrs. Melard, madam. Doctor Diamond is with her, but he's asked that I send for you—and for his wife."

Charlotte and Marilyn rushed to the Melard suite, which was just down the corridor from the dining room. The door was slightly ajar, and they could hear the sobbing as they approached. As they drew close to the cabin door, Captain Jorgenson, with a wild look in

121

his eyes, rushed out of the cabin and turned toward the center foyer of the boat.

Doris Melard was lying on the bed, with Chance crouched over her. Malcolm was sitting in a tub chair off to the side, moaning and sobbing and rocking back and forth, almost uncontrollably. Marilyn went straight to Malcolm, leaned down and wrapped her arms around his shoulders, and started to whisper in his ear. Charlotte walked directly to the bed.

She could clearly see it for herself, but Chance pronounced it as soon as Charlotte reached his side. "She's gone. It looks like a heart attack."

Charlotte turned to Pierre, who was standing and trembling at the door.

"Please bring Detective Frieden here. And, as you did with me, make it as unobtrusive as possible, please. We don't want to alert or frighten the other passengers."

* * * *

Marilyn and Franz Frieden were leaning over Malcolm Melard, Marilyn comforting the man and Frieden trying to be as sensitive as possible in asking him the questions he was required to ask. Charlotte was using what moments she had alone with Chance to ask him questions she had.

"No, I can't be sure that it was a heart attack. But I can't be surprised, either," Chance said in answer to one of Charlotte's questions. "And yes, now that she's gone, I can say that she was sicker than I was letting on. Both she and her husband—but mostly Mrs. Melard—insisted that she didn't care if she died soon but that she wanted this one last cruise—especially that slow float through the Lorelei gorge this morning. She had said back in Nürnberg that she wanted to live to see the castles along the Rhine in this stretch one more time—that she didn't want to die in a Nürnberg hospital. I know I should have insisted, but I could see she was dying, and, frankly, I saw no harm to her or anyone else to help her get her wish. Malcolm said he held her in his lap on a chair over there at the glass doors to the balcony as they cruised the Lorelei gorge and that she was happy that she had been able to hold on that long."

"That's fine," Charlotte said. "I'll not second guess you or anyone else on a decision like that. Just tell Franz Frieden what you have told me when he questions you. He's a fair man, I've observed. It should be fine. There will probably be questions, but if those were obviously her wishes. . . . It would have helped if someone other than you and Professor Melard knew those were her wishes."

"Captain Jorgenson knew—and so did Dietrich Hahn. I could see that it might be a problem if she didn't make it to the end of the cruise. So, I brought Captain Jorgenson in to talk to her. Ultimately, it was his decision more than mine, or even the Melards'. Doris wrote a check to the cruise line—and, yes, I saw that it wasn't made out to Captain Jorgenson personally—and the decision was made beyond the Melards and me to let her remain on the cruise."

"Good. That was good thinking, Chance. I'll make a detective out of you yet. But I also have to ask you about Malcolm Melard. I uncovered rumors that she might be considering divorcing him, and her money would be seen as motive. Did you see, or do you suspect—?"

"I saw nothing but a grieving husband trying everything he could to keep her alive to get her wish, Charlotte. He's in a bad way over this. I certainly hope the authorities don't go after him."

"We'll have to see how that plays out, Chance. Your testimony should help him. But I must tell you that, in what little I did in looking at the situation, I found that, though those involved seem to think this scenario sets up well for a perfect crime, it is fairly common for spouses to be murdered on cruises like this far from home and their usual doctor in what is made to look like natural causes in an attempt to hide the crime. Malcolm is probably lucky that Franz Frieden is already on the scene and he doesn't have to face doubting local authorities he's never met. In any case, Frieden is outside Franz's jurisdiction. His authority beyond his territory only extended to the robberies. He will be as much a bystander here as we are—although probably an influential one."

Captain Jorgenson had returned. "We're pulling into the Koblenz slip just now—nearly thirty minutes before our scheduled landing, but I received permission to expedite the docking because of this emergency," he said. "And I've alerted the authorities. They will meet the vessel at the pier."

"I think I can hear the sirens now," Marilyn said.

"The authorities here are very efficient," Frieden answered.

"About that, Franz, could I have a word?" She pulled him off to the side and briefly sketched out the circumstances and solicited his help with the Koblenz authorities.

As they were speaking, though, a crew member had arrived and was urgently whispering in Captain Jorgensen's ear.

"Doctor Diamond," the captain turned and blurted out, obviously in considerable distress. "Could you come down to the next deck, please. I'm told that another passenger—Bernard Colson—is having a heart attack."

* * * *

Charlotte and Brenda were sitting in the lounge—trying out yet another day's worth of drink specials, Charlotte sipping on a Black Russian and Brenda trying to figure out the ingredients of her Swan Lake—and watching the sunset over the rooftops of the eastern bank of the Rhine and the ridge-hugging walls of the Ehrenbreitstein Castle.

After the bodies of Doris Melard and Bernard Colson had been taken off the ship, the authorities initially questioned Malcolm Melard and Sean Richards and then escorted them off the *Rhine Maiden* as well. Franz Frieden left the vessel with Melard and Richards to help in the enquiries. While this was transpiring, the passengers were confined to the dining room. Eventually, the passengers were permitted to take their scheduled tour in Koblenz, which was a walking tour.

For once, Hattie Timmons had declared to all about her in the dining room that the city tours for this cruise were both too taxing—that they should have easier versions for passengers like her, who were old and walked with canes—and too dull, and had said she would be spending the afternoon being Florence Nightingale to her sick friend,

Irene Summersdale—who, although a great weight on her own forbearance, was, Hattie charged, being treated quite shabbily by an uncaring ship's crew.

Chance and Marilyn had also stayed back, and Charlotte and Brenda had done so as well to help the Diamonds pack. Chance was needed for the medical enquiries, because he had been the attending physician at the deaths of both Doris Melard and Bernard Colson. Having learned that Marilyn was a minister and had counseled both Malcolm Melard and Sean Richards at the times of their loved ones' deaths, she was also permitted to attend the enquiries—and to comfort the men during the process. The authorities had promised that they would see that the Diamonds rejoined the cruise at its end in Amsterdam in just a few day's time.

Hearing a commotion in the foyer reception area, Charlotte rose and walked out into that space. Captain Jorgenson was standing at the open doorway to the top of the gang plank and was reaming out the ship's officer who was on duty there to control the entry and egress from the ship.

"We were told to let none of the passengers except the Diamonds take their luggage off the ship," Charlotte heard Captain Jorgenson spitting out as she approached the two men.

"Have we been able to control what that woman does since she came aboard?" was the duty officer's reply.

"What's gone wrong now?" Charlotte asked as she joined the two.

"That Miss Timmons," Jorgenson said. "She and Miss Summersdale just managed to disembark with all of their luggage. Will the incidents never stop happening on this cruise?"

"I blame it all on my brother," Charlotte said, half amused, thinking on the "doomed vacation" record of Chance, and not in the least upset to have seen the last of Hattie Timmons.

"Excuse me?" Jorgenson said, turning his full attention on Charlotte.

"Never mind. It's a family joke of mine. But, I suggest that you just report the departure to the authorities and not worry about it anymore. If they think they need Hattie Timmons, they can track her down. She's of no consequence to any of this—more of interest to you, I think, in the long run."

"What? Why is that so?" Jorgenson now asked.

"In my checking up on the passengers in recent days, I discovered that Hattie Timmons told us the truth about herself from the very beginning and we just laughed it off."

"I don't understand."

"At the captain's welcome dinner, when we were all revealing our professions, and you noted that Hattie was the most frequent cruiser on this run, she told us she was a professional traveler. She is just that. I discovered that she is a customer service investigator for your own cruise line. I don't know why she's left the boat short of the end of the cruise, but I can tell you that any mystery she's connected with on this cruise solely has to do with grading your crew's service."

"*Scheiss*," Jorgenson blurted out.

"Well said," Charlotte intoned, with a smile.

Chapter Nine: Day Ten, New Year's: Cologne

"Do you think either of the men will rejoin the cruise in Amsterdam tomorrow?"

"No, I don't think either one will, Brenda," Charlotte answered. "Malcolm Melard won't because he is grief stricken and will accompany his wife's body back to Pennsylvania for burial—and Sean Richards certainly won't because he will be in a German jail awaiting trial."

"So, you think that Sean murdered Bernard but that Malcolm had nothing to do with his wife's death?"

"Yes, it was my inclination anyway, but Chance convinced me on both counts. And this was just like what we experienced with the robberies earlier. An inconvenience for what someone saw as a clever plot. Doris's natural death was an inconvenience for Bernard's unnatural one, I think. Something Sean did not foresee in his calculations. It brought immediate attention and suspicion to his murder plot."

"I can see that, yes. An inconvenient death. But how did Chance help focus you on the difference between the two deaths?" Brenda asked. "They were both seen as heart attacks, weren't they? And this after it was thought Irene Summersdale might be having one too."

The two women were standing on the top, open deck of the *Rhine Maiden*, bundled up in every layer of clothes they could put on and still waddle around. They were standing close to each other in an embrace. The two had just watched the awesome midnight New Year's fireworks display over the Rhine where they were docked in the center of Cologne die down. The Germans really knew how to light up New Year's, they both had repeatedly said through barrage after barrage of skyrockets, their beauty enhanced by their reflection over the surface of the river. Both women had also noted several times how much better fireworks were over water than on land.

"Having three heart attack alarms in quick succession was quite an inconvenience for Sean," Charlotte said. "As far as Chance is concerned, he confirmed what my research into the Melards had already indicated to me. There were rumors that Doris was thinking of getting a divorce. But she had been married so often that she probably always was thinking of her next divorce. But Malcolm, in the research, didn't come up as anything but a devoted husband. Malcolm had only been married once before—for a good twenty years, and he had home cared for his wife, who was sinking for some time into the effects of Alzheimer, until she had to be institutionalized. And then the nursing home staff told Margaret Fancel, who was doing the research for me, that he was constantly with his first wife until the end. It just didn't

129

seem like he was the type to be offing his second wife. He wasn't rich, as she was, but he had a comfortable salary as a university professor. Chance's description of the concern he was showing for Doris on the cruise bore that out."

"And Sean Richards?"

"Chance had the key to that too. He didn't tell me of his concern, considering patient privilege to go that far—and he was quite distraught when I told him the importance of the information he had—but I assured him that it was doubtful that it would have meant enough to me at the time for me to prevent Colson's death. Sean Richards kept making sure that people were getting the impression that Colson was ill—and that it was his heart. That did irritate me, but I didn't consider that he had a motive for doing that other than wanting sympathy for how solicitous he was to Colson. The night that Sean went for medicine, saying it was a heart pill Bernard had failed to take, Chance had gone over and talked to Colson. Colson, however, said it was just a sleeping pill—that he was having trouble sleeping. If Chance had told me that the difference existed between the two men on how sick Colson was and the extent of that sickness, I might have been more suspicious. And maybe not."

"What convinced you, though?"

"It was, first, research again. I checked Bernard Colson out on the Internet—which is where, as I told you, I found that he wrote gay novels. I also found that he lived in Connecticut. And then, through Margaret's research, I found that Bernard and Sean were legally married—that they could do that in Connecticut, which no doubt was why they lived in Connecticut. That gave me motive for Sean. He was tired of living as essentially Bernard's indentured companion but he was not tired of Bernard's money. As Bernard's legal spouse, he would inherit it all. After Bernard died, Margaret invoked FBI interest to call Bernard's doctor in the States, who said nothing had been found to be wrong with Bernard's heart—that an old leg wound from falling off a horse made him walk with a cane, but, other than that, he was healthy as a horse. And that, no, the doctor hadn't prescribed heart or sleep pills for him. Added to Chance's observation that Sean was probably lying about Bernard's condition—and the morphine vials they found in the lining to the French purse Sean always carried, a drug that can induce a heart attack—that means the Germans have a very good case against Sean, I'm afraid."

They were silent for a moment, enjoying the lights on the Ehrenbreitstein Castle ramparts.

After a few minutes Brenda laughed one of her twinkling laughs.

"What is it? What do you find funny?"

"I was just thinking of that dreadful Hattie Timmons. It's amusing to find out that she was on the cruise to test out the service. I feel sorry for the *Rhine Maiden*'s crew for having to be evaluated by her."

"Yes, that's something to remember about the trip," Charlotte agreed. "But it turns out she wasn't at all dreadful. Captain Jorgenson tells me that she gave his crew an A plus rating. That she complimented them all on how well and politely they handled everything she threw at them, acknowledging that she had tested them beyond reasonable limits. And I found that she left the cruise early because she genuinely was worried about Irene and took her directly to a hospital in Koblenz for a full checkup—and then bundled her back to the States. They didn't find anything wrong with Irene, though, thankfully. And, so, Hattie wasn't such a witch after all."

Brenda sighed and snuggled up closer to Charlotte. "I miss them, you know?"

"Chance and Marilyn?"

"Yes, I can't wait to see them in Amsterdam. Happily, we will have a couple of days there with them before we have to fly back to Maryland. They've been wonderful about our partnership, and I enjoy traveling with them. I can see you do too."

"Never again, though," Charlotte said. "That Chance curse. It happened just as I told you it would. Always a dead body. I understand that the cruise line is giving him a free trip in thanks for all of the doctoring he had to do on a cruise where he was supposed to be just another passenger. But I'll not be taking that cruise with him. Someone is sure to die on the cruise too. Soon the cruise line will see him for the curse that he is."

"Charlotte Diamond," Brenda said with a sharp tone. "The supposed curse didn't happen as you 'guaranteed' it would. I wasn't going to say anything, but since you brought it up, no one died in the first week, and only two have died. You guaranteed three in the first week."

"We haven't reached Amsterdam yet. We could still easily hit the number."

Brenda laughed. "And you no longer are vacationing with Chance. He's not on the boat now."

It was Charlotte's turn to laugh.

Brenda resumed the attack. "You enjoyed this cruise. Don't try to tell me you didn't. And you enjoyed it all the more once it turned into an investigation. You're all aglow now—because it extended to death and murder. You would take this cruise again, if given the chance. And you'd want Chance and Marilyn on the cruise with you. There's that Queen Elizabeth II Southampton to New York cruise Marilyn mentioned she'd like to go on."

"I hate ocean cruises. I get sea sick."

"Just when was the last time you mentioned being sea sick? It was the day we arrived in Nürnberg—before boarding the *Rhine Maiden*. You weren't sea sick the entire time; didn't even mention the possibility. So, don't say a word to me about not enjoying these vacations—even with Chance along."

"I'd go anywhere, vacation or not—to the ends of the earth, if necessary—with you, Brenda," Charlotte whispered.

"So, March in Florida isn't too far?"

"Well, I guess not. Oh, look at that. It's started again. These Germans certainly know how to do a fireworks display."

The two stood there, leaning into each other, arms around the other, watching the second round of fireworks over the Rhine at Cologne.

"It's really late," Brenda said with a sigh. "Shall we stay out here and watch the rest of the fireworks?"

"I think not," Charlotte answered. "Let's go back to the cabin and make fireworks of our own."

Olivia Stowe

Olivia Stowe is a published author under different names and in other dimensions of fiction and nonfiction and lives quietly in a university town with an indulgent spouse and two demanding Siamese cats.

Books By Olivia Stowe

Charlotte Diamond Mysteries

By the Howling

Retired With Prejudice

Coast to Coast

An Inconvenient Death

Other books

Fiddler's Rest

Spirit of Christmas

Chatham Square

24810107R00074

Made in the USA
Lexington, KY
01 August 2013